Patience McKenna Novels
available in
IPL Library of Crime Classics™
Editions

**SWEET,
SAVAGE DEATH**

**WICKED,
LOVING MURDER**

DEATH'S SAVAGE PASSION

JANE HADDAM

WRITING AS ORANIA PAPAZOGLOU

DEATH'S SAVAGE PASSION

IPL Library of Crime Classics
INTERNATIONAL POLYGONICS, LTD.
New York City

Death's Savage Passion

IPL edition
Cover: © Copyright International Polygonics, Ltd. 2001

ISBN 1-55882-036-1
Printed and manufactured in the United States of America
First IPL printing October 2001

10 9 8 7 6 5 4 3 2 1

For Meredith

Death's Savage Passion

ONE

Everybody who comes to New York from somewhere else and does reasonably well at something nobody has any right to expect to do reasonably well at wants to show off. Some people are very, very successful and very, very lucky and get to do their showing off in print. They appear in *People* and *Us* and *Parade*, telling the world why they love Paris and how the fried oysters at Orsini's make a yearly trip to Rome a *must*. The people back home—the adolescent love object whose scorn destroyed an ego for a decade, the supercilious Latin teacher with dire predictions of ditchdigging at the end of the educational amnesty, the thin girl in Villager skirt and sweater sets who thought pudgy old Maria too boring to bother with—receive their comeuppance in photo bleed. Ms. Really Famous smiles for the photographer and imagines the oh-so-superior Sheree Singer, head cheerleader and Most Popular Girl of the Glen Oaks Senior High School Class of '69, stuffing the latest copy of *Cosmopolitan* into the ride seat of the wire grocery cart between Junior's reeking diapers and her own ballooning stomach. Ms. Really Famous has nothing to worry about. The Sheree Singers of this world *always* end up pushing reeking babies around in wire grocery carts.

The rest of us have to work a little longer, try a little harder, or give up and declare a truce. I thought I'd declared a truce long ago. The girls who were my enemies at Emma Willard were now, like me, women in their thirties. With the exception of a Rockefeller cousin who married an English duke and a Pillsbury relative with a large private income and a penchant for opening campy boutiques, they were proper Manhattan matrons with administrative jobs in Wall Street law firms and husbands in brokerage houses. They envied me my height (six feet), my weight (125 pounds) and sometimes my hair (very long, very thick, very blond). They expected me to envy their *lives.* I didn't, but I didn't tell them that. If I ran into them in Saks, I smiled and nodded and said how wonderful it must be to be settled. I intended to be settled in the year 2000, just in time for the coming of the third millennium.

Maybe if I'd had what most Americans call a normal adolescence—small town or moderate-income suburb, coed public high school, four years at the state university—I would never have gotten involved with Sarah English. Maybe I would have been like Phoebe, my old Greyson College roommate and now the world's bestselling author of very, very sexy (almost rude) historical romances. Phoebe changed her name from Weiss to Damereaux, established an affinity for floor-length velvet caftans and multiple strands of rope diamonds, and smiled very determinedly at the cameras. She was content with her press notices. When she went back to Union City, she took long, slow walks to the corner liquor store and waved at all the girls who thought she was fat and impossible in the eleventh grade.

I did not have Union City to fall back on. When things started going too well—when I found myself with a great apartment in a city where apartments had become extinct, when my book was doing well in a market so bad most people were having difficulty getting published, when I woke up every morning next to a good man at a time all the good ones were taken—I had no one to show off *to.* My friends from school thought writing was "irregular," not exciting. Someone with my "connections" was supposed to get married and get serious about raising money for the American Cancer Society. I *needed* someone like Sarah English. I needed the hero worship. I needed the flattery. Most of all, I needed confirmation that I was living an unusual and enviable life. God only knows why.

Unfortunately, at the time I received Sarah's first letter (and her manuscript), I wasn't in the habit of being honest with myself. Even after I had given her battered Xerox to my agent, even after my agent had sold the book to Austin, Stoddard & Trapp, even as Sarah was getting off the 4:15 from New Haven, I still thought I was only trying to *help*. This is how much I was trying to help: Sarah was coming in from Holbrook, Connecticut, to deliver her contracts to Caroline Dooley at AST. I offered her a place to sleep in my apartment (since I have no furniture, I offered a sleeping bag and the floor). I called every romance writer I knew (and I knew them all) and arranged a dinner at Bogie's. I went down to Putumayo and spent $110 on a fuzzy rose and white cardigan to wear with my charcoal gray Ralph Lauren box pleat ("Skidmore") skirt. Even Nick thought I was being excessive.

Phoebe thought I was being ridiculous. Dinner at Bogie's was both sense and nonsense. It was sense because Bogie's was the Elaine's of mystery writing, and Sarah's novel was a romantic suspense ("in the tradition of Mary Stewart," as she said, three times [each] in both her letter to me and her cover letter to the manuscript). It was nonsense because mystery writers are not very happy about romance writers. Mystery writers have a Cause. They write Literature, whether anybody understands that or not. Of course, anybody can join the Mystery Writers of America as an affiliate—MWA's word for a fan—and a number of mystery writers spent the mystery lull and romance boom grinding out pseudonymous "contemporary love stories" for the category lines, but that didn't make relations any easier. A hard-boiled private eye writer named Max Brady (five two, 130, horn-rims) once got into a fistfight with a romance writer named Verna Train outside the Hotel Pierre, either accidentally or deliberately witnessed by two reporters from the *Post* and a camera crew from "The CBS Evening News." Verna won, but that hardly settled the argument.

By the time Sarah arrived in New York, relations between romance writers and mystery writers had disintegrated into a near-open declaration of war. The romance boom was over. The mystery boom was on. Romance lines were looking at 45 percent returns, then 65 percent returns. Simon and Schuster sold Silhouette to Harlequin. Editors made cautious suggestions that the market might—just might—be glutted. The real romance stars—people like Phoebe, and Amelia Samson, and rape-and-ravage-bodice-ripper Lydia Wentward—were eased to hardcover and "midlist." A few hundred bad romance writers started turning out bad mystery novels—sometimes not so bad as the bad mystery novels turned out by bad mystery writers, which meant a lot of bad mystery writers were bumped out of the genre. What was worse, they were bumped by romantic suspense, a bastard genre, a female perversion, a she-serpent in the male Eden created fifty years ago by Chandler and Hammett. Good mystery writers spent a lot of time at the bar in Bogie's, lamenting the *New York Times Book Review*'s lack of seriousness when reviewing crime fiction and suggesting various baroque methods for doing away with whoever had had the bright idea of rereleasing M. M. Kaye's pre-*Far Pavilions* sentimentalized claptrap.

Under the circumstances, it might have been smarter to make reservations for neutral territory, but I couldn't do it. Sarah English had written a romantic suspense novel because she liked romantic suspense novels and hadn't been able to find enough of them. She was right on the money. I saw no reason to pick up the tab for cocktails at the Palm Court and pretend the dying aristocracy would last. I wanted Sarah to see and be seen where it would *matter*. Besides, I wasn't writing romances myself anymore. I was doing true crime (my book on the Agenworth murder, just released, was a weak number fourteen on the *Times* bestseller list). I had an active membership in the MWA, a number of friendly acquaintances among the advocates of classic whodunits, and a growing relationship with Bogie's owners, Billy and Karen Palmer. Also, Bogie's serves very satisfying amounts of very good food at very good prices. Romance writer restaurants serve decorative amounts of suspicious food at ridiculous prices. Bogie's was *perfect*.

Bogie's was even more perfect after I finally saw Sarah English, New Author Extraordinaire. Sarah English was everything a New Yorker could ask for in a small-town hick come to the big city. She was peculiarly out of shape. After a few years in Manhattan most women either let themselves go entirely or develop unnatural relationships with *Jane Fonda's Workout Tape*. Sarah English had done neither. She was thinner than she should have been for her height—eighty pounds on a five-foot frame—but she was soft, almost liquid, lumpy. She was actually wearing lime green polyester and plastic patent leather bow-ribboned shoes. She had her sandy blond hair tortured into a flip.

Phoebe squinted across the Grand Concourse of Grand Central Station—we were meeting Sarah "under the clock"—and nearly fainted dead away.

"Good God," she said. "You can't take that into *Bogie's.*"

"Of course I can take her into Bogie's," I said. "Billy and Karen aren't prejudiced."

"I'm not talking about Billy and Karen." She got her pearl-handled lorgnette out of her blue velvet string bag and peered into the middle distance like a society woman in a Marx Brothers movie. She shook her head. "Maybe it's the wrong person," she said. "Maybe—"

"She looks just like she sounds on the phone."

She behaved just the way she sounded on the phone. Halfway across the concourse she stopped, stared at the clock over the information booth, and rubbed the top of her left foot against the stocking on her right leg. She bit her lip. She fumbled in her handbag (imitation patent leather, lime green) and came up with a card.

"Maybe I ought to go get her," I said.

Phoebe held me back. "This is the biggest indoor clock in the Western world," she said, "and if that woman can't see it—"

Sarah English had seen it. She had seen us, too. She let her face be taken over by an open-lipped smile (gap between her front teeth, gold filling in her right incisor), and started hurrying toward us. She stopped a foot and a half away.

"Oh," she said. "Oh, you look just like I *wanted* you to."

Phoebe (Weiss) Damereaux has no patience for fools, liars, or idiots, but she is a kindhearted woman. She could no more have looked on Sarah English with indifference than she could have left a wounded cat in the road. Sarah English was so eager, so naive, and so very, painfully plain. I looked at her and knew she had spent the past thirty-five years in cramped, badly painted apartments, slowly turning into the town old maid. Sarah English was one of those not quite middle-aged ladies to whom nothing had ever happened and nothing ever would—except something had. *We* had happened to her. New York had happened to her. Austin, Stoddard & Trapp had happened to her. She was ugly and pitiable and under any other circumstances would have been impossible to bear. These were not, however, other circumstances. This was a success story.

Phoebe grabbed Sarah English's hand and pumped it, hard.

"I'm Phoebe Damereaux," she said. "This is—"

"Oh, I know," Sarah English said. "This is *Patience Campbell McKenna.*" She said "Patience Campbell McKenna" the way devout Roman Catholics say "Blessed Virgin Mary." I blushed. I hadn't blushed since I was six.

"McKenna," I said finally. "Everybody just calls me Mc-Kenna."

"*I* call you Patience," Phoebe said.

"Only when you're drunk," I said.

Sarah English obviously thought this was the way New York women talked. She was delighted.

"I've read all about both of you in the papers," she said. "About how Miss McKenna solves murders and Miss Damereaux sells so many books and has such an unusual apartment, and of course pictures of Mr. Carras—he's *so* good-looking—and of course I modeled my heroine on *you,* Miss McKenna—"

I closed my eyes. It was beginning to occur to me just what I'd been after when I invited Sarah English to New York. It's not a terrible thing to want admiration, but enough is enough. Sarah's blind worship was making me uncomfortable.

"Just McKenna," I told her. "Not *Miss* McKenna, just Mc-Kenna. Or Pay. It comes of having spent my early life in girls' schools. Also, it's getting to be rush hour, and if we intend to get up to my apartment and then down to Bogie's by seven—"

Phoebe shot me a look that said she knew exactly what I was thinking and why. She put an arm around Sarah's shoulders and patted her comfortingly.

"Patience is right," she said. "If we want to get a cab—"

"Oh, I want to get a cab," Sarah English said. "I've been dying to ride in a real New York cab."

The look Phoebe gave me this time was murderous. Three days with Sarah English might be wonderful or awful, but it was certainly going to be a responsibility. I had an almost irresistible urge to tell the woman that the garbagemen were making forty thousand a year and hankering to strike for more, that the streets hadn't been cleaned since June, that the mugging rate was down but the burglary rate up—anything to tone down her conviction that Madison Avenue was paved with platinum and fairy dust— not angel dust—grew every Christmas on the tree in Rockefeller Center. I would have had to shut her up first.

"I just kept sending that manuscript and sending that manuscript," she was saying. "I sent it to all the publishing houses and all the agents in the *Writer's Market* and all the writers I'd ever heard of, mystery writers and romance writers and everyone, and of course I was afraid to send it to Miss McKenna, Miss McKenna is a detective, not just a writer, but in the end there was nothing else to do, and—"

"There's a cab stand right out front," Phoebe said. "We'll go up to the West Side and then—"

I never did find out what we were going to do "then." Sarah English couldn't stop talking. She talked all the way out to Forty-second Street. She talked while we were getting into the cab. She was still talking thirty odd streets later, when we got out of it. She talked while I was hauling her brown plastic suitcase onto the sidewalk

When she went back to give the cabbie a little extra tip, she kissed him on the nose.

TWO

Karen Palmer was standing in the doorway when we drove up to Bogie's in Sarah's second New York cab. She had her hands in her hair and her eyes on the sky, as if looking for rain. New Yorkers do a lot of this. I have never been able to figure out what for.

She saw me unfolding on the sidewalk (my legs are so long I am required to unfold from all cars except Checker cabs, stretch limousines, and Rolls-Royce Corniches) and came over to help.

"There you are," she said. "You can take care of it."

"Take care of what?" Sarah was shaking out the wrinkles in her lilac nylon date dress, shifting from one foot to the other on out-of-season lilac plastic sandals. I looked at her dubiously. It was mid-October. Bogie's is at Twenty-sixth and Eighth, not a bad neighborhood, but not a tourist neighborhood either. Sarah might as well have had a neon sign saying "Out-of-Towner" bolted to her forehead. I half expected a souvenir hustler, radar always on the alert, to beam himself down from Forty-second Street and clobber her over the head with an "I Love New York" bumper sticker. If she hadn't looked so happy, I would have clobbered her myself.

Karen Palmer looked worried.

"Max Brady is at the bar," she said. "Your friend Verna is in a corner. They can see each other through the archway."

"Oh, shit," I said.

"Max Brady is getting plastered," Karen Palmer said.

Sarah English looked at us brightly. The "shit" that would have been an insult from her local newsboy was a mark of sophistication in New York. She stared at Karen Palmer, fascinated. Karen was in an ordinary pair of jeans and doing nothing particularly unusual, but that didn't stop Sarah. Karen has a Lauren Bacall voice. That might have explained it. I mentally gave the problem of Sarah English to Phoebe and tried to concentrate on something I could understand. Max Brady getting plastered a hundred feet from Verna Train, and the ramifications thereof, I could understand.

I just didn't like it.

"I think it's under control," Karen said. "He's with DeAndrea, and DeAndrea doesn't drink."

"Billy should be able to take care of Max Brady," I said.

We both looked toward the door, contemplating Billy with an armlock on Max Brady. Max Brady being Max Brady, Tweety Pie could have got an armlock on him.

"Billy doesn't want to take care of Max Brady," Karen said. "At least, not like that." She gave Sarah and Phoebe a big smile and said, "Everybody else is already here. They look great."

They did look great. As soon as we got to the archway, I spotted them, spread across two tables in the far corner of the dining room and arrayed like peacocks during the mating season. Amelia Samson had come in vintage Worth, every inch of her stout, well-muscled body covered with beaded satin so stiff it could have stood on its own if she'd climbed out of it. Marilou Saunders (hostess of "Wake Up and Shine! America," a talk show for people who think dawn is *not* a four-letter word) was rigged out as a forties tramp, complete with red spangled bolero jacket, red plastic barrette, stiletto heels, and a black satin skirt slit up the side of her thigh to her waist. Verna Train, who wrote "long" (nonline) contemporary romances and looked like the middle-aged John Barrymore in drag, was sporting a two-foot-long ebony and silver cigarette holder. Next to this outpouring of pride in the genus feminine, the publishing women looked almost drab. Dana Morton, my agent and now Sarah's, was New York thin and New York chic in a plain black wool loaded down with "accessories" (Charivari bullet belt, Hermes red "spring" scarf, silver bangles). Caroline Dooley, Sarah's editor at AST, was businesslike in a gray flannel suit and tiny gold earrings.

Max Brady was in blue jeans and a shapeless crew neck he must have had in college. He had his back to the dining room.

One of the reasons romance writers have little respect for mystery writers is that, in romance writer terms, mystery writers don't know how to "promote themselves." Max Brady took that truism a step further. He didn't know how to match his socks.

I let Phoebe and Sarah go in without me and climbed onto a stool next to William L. DeAndrea, two-time Edgar winner (an Edgar is like an Oscar, except it's given by the Mystery Writers of America instead of the Motion Picture Association to a mystery novel instead of a movie) and all around Nice Person. DeAndrea was so optimistic, he didn't have to bother trying to think well of people. He thought well of people. He thought well of a lot of people who had no right being thought well of.

"I've got a romance title for you," he said. *"Starved for Love,* by Anna Rexia."

"Tell me about it," I said.

"How about *Plunging Passions,* by Dee Fenestrate."

"You could do that with mystery novels," I said. *"Death on Vacation,* by Maura Torium."

"Not bad."

Billy Palmer was behind the bar. I signaled for a Perrier to match DeAndrea's. I'd go to work on the Drambuie *after* dinner.

"I wanted to talk to you about *that,"* I said, making what I hoped was a covert gesture at Max. "That is going to be a problem."

"That is already a problem," DeAndrea said. "That is stewed. In fact, that is soon to be sick."

"Oh, fine," I said. "Under the circumstances—"

"Under the circumstances, I don't think you have anything to worry about. You would if the mess his book is in were the main problem, but it isn't."

"Lisa left him. Again."

"Third time this month."

"What kind of a mess is his book in?"

DeAndrea shrugged. "He writes hard-boiled California private eye, his book is in a mess. Nobody reads that stuff anymore. At least nobody reads people like Max. He had a twenty-five-hun-dred-dollar advance and it's being remaindered without earning even that back. *My Rod Is Hot.* That one. AST doesn't even want to talk to him anymore."

"He really wrote a book called *My Rod Is Hot?*"

I looked over my shoulder at the table in the corner and Caroline Dooley in her gray flannel suit. "AST," I said.

"Yeah," DeAndrea said. "Not that she didn't say hello. She was very polite."

"Oh, fine," I said.

"The problem is, I don't read that stuff either."

I made another gesture in Max's direction. "Can he hear any of this?"

"Right now he couldn't hear Big Ben if it went off under his earlobe."

On the far stool, Max Brady suddenly sat up and said, in a very sober, clear, and portentous voice: "Raymond Chandler is the only serious writer to emerge from Depression America."

Billy Palmer gave him a worried look. You are allowed to get only so drunk and no drunker in New York State. Max might very well have crossed the line. It was hard to tell. Max Brady was the kind of drunk who looked and sounded sober until he fell to the floor and passed out.

I slid off my stool, stretched, and patted DeAndrea on the arm. "Get him out of here," I said. "If he starts another fight with Verna, she's going to break a chair over his head."

"If he starts another fight with Verna, *I'm* going to break a chair over his head," DeAndrea said. "Then again, maybe I'll let Verna do it. She can afford it better than I can."

At the table in the corner, Sarah was high, Verna was cool, Phoebe was gracious. The rest of them were a little stiff, as if they weren't sure how they felt about each other. They parodied themselves. Dana made noises about sub rights and paperback deals. Marilou giggled lewdly. Amelia harrumphed. Caroline Dooley held a molded crystal paperweight in the air, explaining to no one in particular that it was really her initials and the most marvelous present anyone had ever given her. Sarah was launched on her fifteenth retelling of the Story of the Miracle.

"I sent that novel to everybody," she said. "I even sent it to all of *you.*"

Verna Train looked down her nose and her cigarette holder, making her eyes cross. "What did you say your name was again?"

"Sarah English," Sarah said. She blinked, but she wasn't annoyed. She didn't expect anyone really famous, like Verna Train, to remember her name.

"Never heard of you," Verna Train said.

"I sent it care of your publishing company," Sarah said.

I took the seat beside her and patted her on the shoulder, in almost conscious imitation of Phoebe.

"Ninety percent of the people you sent that thing to never got it," I said. "Ninety percent of the people who got it didn't read it. *I* didn't read it."

Sarah English looked shocked. "But you helped me get it published," she said. She flushed, eying Caroline Dooley. "Accepted for publication," she corrected herself. "How could you help me if you didn't read it?"

"I sent it along to Dana," I said. "Dana read it. If Dana hated it, I'd have read it to see if I wanted to work on it, but Dana loved it, and Caroline loved it, and here you are."

"It's so complicated," Sarah said.

Actually, it wasn't complicated at all. It's both easier and harder to get published than most people think. Easier, because writing commercial fiction is a game with rules written down in a number of places, and because the vaunted "slush piles" mostly contain manuscripts so excrutiatingly terrible they don't even constitute competition. Harder, because a new writer without friends or contacts is like odd man out at a square dance. She has to find a way to join the circle. There *are* ways, but finding them isn't easy.

Caroline Dooley wiped Bloody Mary off her upper lip and said, "Some of it's luck. We were looking hard for good romantic suspense. You gave us good romantic suspense. We could have been looking hard for stories about cats."

"Maybe I'll write a romantic suspense about cats," Verna said. "I have cats."

"All romance writers have cats," Phoebe said.

At the far side of the table, Amelia sighed. "Romantic suspense, romantic suspense," she said. "Blood and guts and people tied up in basements. Who wants all that stuff?"

"You're writing a whole romantic suspense *line*," Verna said.

Amelia sniffed. "Money's money," she said. "I still don't know who wants all that stuff."

"Everybody wants that stuff," Verna Train said. "Maybe you and Phoebe can do anything you want to, but the rest of us have to pay attention to the market."

"I always pay attention to the market," Amelia said.

"But you don't have to," Verna said. "You don't have to do things you—" She stopped and looked into her drink. The rest of us, suddenly quiet, looked into her drink with her.

In the corner, Marilou Saunders rustled her clothes and giggled. "I wrote a romantic suspense," she said. She giggled again and waved her drink in the air, something that looked like straight Scotch. The rest of us turned away from her. Marilou was a pill and cocaine addict—at least we thought she was—and when she was high, she was impossible. When we insisted, she left her paraphernalia at home, but she always stoked up before walking out the door. We couldn't do anything about her and we'd given up trying.

Verna had given up listening. "I don't even like romantic suspense," she was saying. "I mean, I wrote one—"

"You wrote a wonderful one," Caroline Dooley said. "I heard from Sheila over at Gallard Rowson. She's very impressed."

"Yeah," Verna said. She tapped her nails against her glass, inexplicably at a loss. "Well," she started up again, "I'm a professional. A professional should be able to do what she's asked to do. I just don't like the stuff, that's all. I don't want to spend the next twenty years embroiling my heroines in smuggling plots. I want to concentrate on *love*."

"We want you to concentrate on love, too," Caroline said. "For God's sake, Verna, this is a fad. Give it a year or two. Less."

"In the meantime, I either go bankrupt or crazy."

"I just like to imagine myself having adventures," Sarah said. "That's what I did with my book, *Shadows in the Light.*"

"*Shadows in the Light?*" Verna said. "That's the name of your book?"

"Don't you think it's a good title?" Sarah said. "I thought it was a wonderful title, but—"

"I'm not criticizing your title," Verna said.

This time, when Sarah flushed, there was a little anger in it. Verna was being rude. I was glad to see Sarah getting just tiddly enough on gin and tonics and just accustomed enough to this table to think she didn't have to put up with Verna's rudeness forever. Of course, since Verna was invariably rude, I didn't see what good it was going to do Sarah to take offense at it.

"I just like to imagine what it would be like to lead an interesting life," Sarah said, her voice steady and surprisingly strong. "I live in this small town. People who live in New York just can't realize. I go to work in an office every day and sometimes I go to a movie with women friends, and once a year I go on a package tour for vacation, if I can afford it. Mostly, I can't afford it. People in New York just don't realize how much people in places like Holbrook want to escape from that."

Caroline Dooley came as close as I'd ever heard her to laughing out loud. "Oh yes we do," she said. "That's why Miss Samson over there has enough money to buy New Jersey."

"Nobody in their right mind," Amelia said, "wants to buy New Jersey."

"If I had enough money to buy New Jersey, I'd wait out the market until people were buying what I want to write," Verna said. She waved her cigarette holder in the air. "Two years ago I got a divorce—from a psychiatrist, yet—and I turned down the alimony, I turned down the property settlement, I walked away with my nose in the air. I'm a romance writer, right? *Now* look at me."

"You're hardly starving," Dana said.

Sarah English was frowning in concentration. "Men are all right," she said, "but they just aren't enough. I mean, there are men in Holbrook. And what would be the use of marrying the world's handsomest and richest man if you were just going to live like every other housewife in Holbrook?"

"That doesn't make any sense," Verna said. "The point about housewives in Holbrook is they don't have any money."

"The point about housewives in Holbrook," Marilou Saunders said, "is they don't have any *sex.*"

"The point about housewives in Holbrook is that they're housewives," Sarah said. Her voice positively rang. *This* she was sure of. "I used to read about Miss McKenna in the papers," she gave me an adoring look. I wondered how long it was going to take to talk her out of that "Miss." "I used to think what an exciting life she had, mixed up in murders, and helping the police, and writing books, and living in New York, and having a lover—"

I nearly choked on my Perrier. Sarah had found out Nick was my lover from the newspapers? My mother, charity queen of Fairfield County, was going to *kill* me.

"I wanted to have a life just like that," Sarah was saying, "as different from Holbrook as possible and nothing like a housewife. I mean, you have to admit, housewives don't get to do anything. Even if they like being housewives, it has to get boring."

"I was a housewife once," Amelia said. "I wouldn't say it was boring."

"You couldn't say it was pleasant, either," I reminded her.

"You should see the book I'm working on now," Sarah said. "My heroine's pulling off a diamond heist and she's got a good reason for it and it's exciting. It's something different. Of course, there's sex in it, they make you put sex in it, but I think most people are like me and skip those parts. I mean, nobody believes that stuff."

"I do," Phoebe said. She looked wistful. She had built her reputation on the hottest sex scenes in the business ("good parts" as they're known among the fans). She was addicted to the self-help section of the Fifth Avenue Barnes & Noble.

Amelia had built her reputation on syrupy sixty-thousand-word tracts (one a *week* for the past thirty years), all of which ended with the closing of the wedding-night bedroom door. She thought Sarah was right on the mark.

"Miss English has a point," she said. "Men have never been a tenth as good as we hoped or a hundredth as good as they think they are."

Verna Train looked depressed.

THREE

I made it home earlier than the rest of them. *They* wanted to do a round of bars—a singles place on the West Side outfitted entirely in pink, a chrome and stained-glass hockey pub (East Side) where all the tables were miniature aquariums filled with yellow-striped tropical fish, a blues place in the Forties where the waiters wore bow-tie earrings and Little Orphan Annie decoder rings. Phoebe, who is president of the American Writers of Romance, was deep in conversation with Dana about returns accounting and warranty clauses. Caroline was showing her molded crystal paperweight around for the sixth time. Verna was morose. Sarah wanted to see more of New York. Amelia had a serious gin gleam in her eye. When Amelia gets a serious gin gleam, she can lay waste to Gordon's principal warehouse. *I* had had three double Drambuies and decided I was either going to get home to sanity or melt. I dropped Sarah and Phoebe at the Forties blues place and went uptown.

When I opened the door to my apartment, the cat was waiting in the foyer and every light in every one of the twelve rooms was blazing. I live in the Braedenvoorst, one of those New York apartment buildings more famous than most of the people living in it, in an apartment willed to me by a romance writer named Myrra Agenworth. Myrra also willed me "everything in the apartment at the time of [her] death" and her story, which was the start of the book I now had on the bestseller list (barely on, but on). I did better with the story than I did with the apartment. After I sold all the furniture and the paintings at auction at Sotheby's (with the exception of Myrra's portrait, which I kept over the fireplace in the living room), I banked the money to pay the maintenance. Then I neglected to buy new furniture. I had a platform bed, a night table, a worktable, a kitchen table, and five chairs. That was it. In twelve rooms.

I put the cat on the kitchen table and went to the refrigerator to see if there were socks in it. Nick always keeps his clean socks in the refrigerator. He usually keeps them in *my* refrigerator because I have a built-in washer-dryer, which is what he uses to do laundry. He rolls his socks into balls, so they look like blackened melons against the white enamel. Then he turns on all the lights and waits in the one bedroom with a bed in it.

The socks were in the otherwise empty vegetable bin. There were five balled pairs of them, arranged in a pyramid. I kicked the drawer shut, got a can of decaffeinated Diet Coke and the container of Devon cream, and started searching cabinets for a saucer. Nick, my cleaning lady, and I all put away dishes in my apartment. We each have strongly held views on where they belong.

I found two saucers in what I thought of as my silverware drawer, filled one with Devon cream and the other with dry cat food, and put them both on the floor. Camille licked at the Devon cream and sat in the cat food.

My mail and my appointment calendar (a bound composition book with the date written at the top of each page in Bic medium point) were on the kitchen table. Tomorrow I had to go to Austin, Stoddard & Trapp (who had paperback rights to my Agenworth book) to discuss possible promotion with an escapee from Hunter College named Evelyn Nesbitt Kleig. I had to meet Dana and "get things straightened out," by which she meant come to my senses and accept the miniseries offer. I also had a session at a place called Images, but I was trying to forget it.

The mail was considerably less exciting: an envelope from the Mystery Writers of America that was undoubtably their monthly publication, *The Third Degree;* three bills (Saks, Bonwit's, and, God help me, Bloomingdale's), none of which I had any intention of looking at for at least a week; and a letter from Dana's office with "J. Dunby, Foreign Rights" written under the letterhead. I opened that one. Four hundred thirty dollars for the Yugoslavian rights to *Love's Dangerous Journey,* the last romance novel I wrote for the now defunct Fires of Love line at Farret Paperback Originals.

I wandered across my empty living room and through the back hall, turning off lights.

"Listen," I said. "I want you to sue someone for me."

No answer. I went into the bedroom and found Nick sitting cross-legged in the middle of my bed, stacks of word-processor printed pages (right-hand margin justification) arranged artfully on my grandmother's wedding quilt. He had a Walkman around his neck and earphones in his ears. I took the earphones away from him, listened for thirty seconds to the Beach Boys doing *Be True to Your School,* and tossed them aside.

"I want you to sue someone for me," I said again.

"Who is it this time?" He cleared a space for me on the bed. I sat down in it.

"The Mystery Writers of America," I said. "For sex discrimination."

"This is number nine," he said. "In the last six months."

"Which means what?"

"Which means in the last six months you have asked me to sue nine separate organizations for sex discrimination, including the American Kennel Club. If I remember rightly, you objected to pick-of-the-litter rules. For God's sake, McKenna, you don't even own a dog."

"Not the point," I said.

"Exactly the point," he said. "Also, you told me the MWA had a whole slew of female directors, or officers, or whatever they are."

"That's not the *point* either," I said.

"What is the point? How do you sue an organization for sex discrimination when half their officers are female?"

"Romantic suspense," I said. "They hate romantic suspense."

"I hate romantic suspense," Nick said. "But Patience. Remember: recourse to law. Sex discrimination is bad, I don't approve of it, but there is a difference between what is and what is not a situation to which the proper response is recourse to law. I sued the telephone company for you, didn't I?"

"Not for sex discrimination."

"Never mind what we called it when we went to court. It was sex discrimination. You wanted the policy changed, I got the policy changed. Right?"

"Right," I said. I fished a cigarette out of my bag.

"Quit," he said.

"What?" The lighter was defunct. I started hunting for matches. Camille, brown and gray kernels of dry cat food clinging to her fur, jumped onto the bed and started playing with the Walkman earphones. It took her exactly one third of a second to tie her paws into immobility.

Nick started to untangle her. "Quit," he said again. "If you don't like it, for whatever reason that may be, quit."

"Well, no," I said. "Where would I hear the gossip?"

"This is about gossip?" Nick said.

"Well," I said.

"Don't quit," Nick said. "Don't sue either. Untie the cat."

I said, "Oh." There wasn't anything else to say. I found a matchbook (Mamma Leone's; Phoebe must have got it for me) and lit up. Nick had all six feet eight inches of himself sprawled across his papers and his hands in Camille's fur. He is a remarkably good-looking man, powerfully built in the shoulders, slender and elegant in the hips. Even Amelia, who ranks men a rung below Godless Communists in the natural order of things, can't resist Nick.

I turned my back to him and lay my head on his chest. "Sorry I'm so contentious," I said. "I've just had five hours of romantic suspense."

"So have I." He gestured to the papers on the bed, then plunged his hands in and came up with a paperback cover proof for a novel called *Dangerous Liaison*. The cover painting showed a man and a woman on a windowsill ledge over a four-story drop. He had his arms around her waist and was bending her backward. She was wearing an off-the-shoulder peasant blouse and four-inch high-heeled sandals.

"Marvelous," I said.

"Romantic suspense and the lack of romantic suspense," he

said. "I'm either putting people into it or filing bankruptcy for people who didn't get out of category romance fast enough. It's all I do anymore."

"Phoebe's bringing you clients," I said.

"Phoebe's bringing me clients," he agreed. "Believe me, I'm grateful. I've got my own office. I'm making enough to get married on, even to you. I will tell you, however, that I'm getting sicker than you'll ever know of romantic suspense."

I ignored the crack about marriage. Nick was always making cracks about marriage.

"I just don't understand it," I said. "Two years ago, three romance lines had hundred-million-dollar years. How could things change so fast?"

"Market saturation and editorial incompetence."

"Thanks."

I felt him shrug. "Right at this moment, every category romance line is in trouble. At least two of them are probably going to crash. If you want my opinion, the romantic suspense lines aren't going to save the situation for long. They're making the same mistakes and they're going to go on making them. Six books a month, twelve books a month, fourteen books a month. Tip sheets, which means all the books start sounding the same after the first year. General conviction that the readers are fools and illiterates and can't tell good from bad. You name it."

"Susan Dangerfield," I said, picking up another cover proof. This one had a man and a woman in a dark alley. He had one arm under her breasts and the other pointing into the distance, a .357 Magnum dangling from his fingers. She was wearing an off-the-shoulder peasant blouse and four-inch high-heeled sandals.

"One of my packagers is thinking of doing a line," Nick said. "This is research."

"What happens when romantic suspense doesn't work?"

"More bankruptcies. A few real disasters. From what I hear, your agent is going to go down like a penny dropping from the observation deck of the World Trade Center."

"Dana?"

"It's just a rumor," Nick said. "They say she's bare-assed to the wind with a storm coming up behind her, and I believe it. Have you seen that line she's doing for Gallard Rowson?" He hunted through his papers. "Passionate Intrigues. That's what it's called. Nothing but brand-name authors. Some minor television celebrities. They have to be costing her ten thousand a shot in up-front. She's going to have to sell a lot of books to justify the expense."

I thought of Verna's romantic suspense, and something clicked.

"That must have been what Verna was talking about at dinner," I said. "She kept complaining about how she wrote a romantic suspense and she hated it, and I couldn't figure out why she bothered."

"She's Dana's client?"

"Yeah."

"Dana probably talked her into it. Circumstances probably talked her into it. She wasn't big enough to survive this thing. She had a little trouble with her last publisher." He shrugged again.

I had a sudden vision of Phoebe thumbing furtively through sex manuals at the back of the Fifth Avenue Barnes & Noble. "Nick?" I said. "Is Phoebe going to be all right? I mean, are her books going to do well, or is she going to get caught up in this thing and find herself having to write juveniles or something?"

"*Wild Winter Passionsong* was number one on the *Times* list for thirty-six weeks."

"That doesn't answer my question."

"Yes it does."

"Nick—"

"That's all you care about, isn't it? You don't know anything about the business you're in and you don't want to know."

"I want to know about Phoebe."

"Phoebe will be all right. Let's change the subject."

"To what?"

"I can think of a lot of things. I can think of some that haven't come up recently."

"That came up two days ago."

"So it's been two days."

"Nick."

"Just letting you know you haven't been forgotten."

I turned over on my stomach, searching for an ashtray. "I'm drunk," I said. "And for your information, I don't care about the business and I don't want to care. I want to write nice long nonfiction books about murders I haven't been involved in and go on Johnny Carson and talk about what psychopaths eat for breakfast. That's all."

"Murders you haven't been involved in."

"Exactly."

He put his hands in my hair and stroked the back of my neck with the tips of his fingers. It was a very comforting gesture, the physical equivalent of a lullaby.

"It'll be all right," he said. "The Agenworth book is successful. The Brookfield book will be successful next year. You'll think of something to do a third book on. A nice historical murder."

"Ancient history," I said.

"Ancient history," he agreed. He stood up and started stacking papers into his arms. "I'll let you sleep," he said. "Dream about Lizzie Borden. You aren't going to get personally involved in any more murders."

It was about five in the morning when Phoebe called to tell me Verna Train was dead.

FOUR

Nick had to be there because he was Phoebe's lawyer, and Amelia's lawyer, and even Caroline Dooley's lawyer—at least he'd been Caroline Dooley's lawyer when she got her divorce, which was the only time she'd needed a lawyer. I didn't have to be there, but I was. Maybe it was Phoebe's voice, sounding so oddly uneven over the phone. Maybe it was the thought of Sarah English, ending her first night on the town in New York in a tangle of police and hysterical women.

They were in the Lexington Avenue subway station at Twenty-third, and *none* of them was hysterical. Dana and Caroline were sitting on a bench, doing their best to look like Good Business-women and Good Citizens. Sarah was sitting on the bench with them, mildly drunk and very, very curious. Amelia was lecturing the police. Phoebe was standing just a little to the side of the one open entrance, waiting for us. I noticed the out-of-place first. Max Brady was standing alone in the middle of the platform, looking pugnacious and panicked at once.

Phoebe and Sarah ran up to us as soon as we came off the stairs. It was odd to see Phoebe in floor-length velvet and forty pounds of jewelry at nearly dawn. Her topknot had come undone. Her wiry hair fell around her face in undisciplined wisps, making her look like an electrified ghost.

Sarah smiled when she saw me, then frowned, then looked near tears. "It isn't the way I expected it would be," she said. She made a mighty effort at cogitation. "Of course, it isn't a *murder.*"

Phoebe ignored her. "I don't know what we're going to do," she said. "They got the train out of here, but I don't know what we're supposed to do *now.*"

"Train?" I half thought she was talking about Verna. We had

been drifting in the direction of Amelia and the police. Nick put a hand on my arm and stopped me.

"I don't think you ought to go over there," he said. "I don't know if you've ever seen one of these, but I have, and it's going to be a *mess.*"

"It is a mess," Phoebe said.

"It's like something out of *The Texas Chainsaw Massacre,*" Sarah said sickly. "There was so much *blood.*"

"What's a mess?" I said. "What does this have to do with a train?"

Phoebe blinked twice, decided I wasn't being willfully perverse, and said, "That's what happened. Verna fell off the platform and got hit by a train. The Lexington Avenue local."

I stepped back, a jerky, involuntary, instinctive reaction that did nothing to calm the sudden, violent churning in my stomach. There had been a subway accident scene in a god-awful Z movie Nick and I had seen in Times Square, a scene full of blood and metal and hanging intestines. I looked over my shoulder at the tracks. Through the knot of police I could see a smear of blood on the far wall, nothing else. I didn't need anything else. If I could have made myself move, I would have been sick.

"I'll go over and talk to them," Nick said. "Sit down, for God's sake."

We didn't sit down. We stood watching him cross the platform. Then we turned away and stared at the graffiti on the wall behind the bench. I got a pack of cigarettes out of my pocket, extracted and lit one. I have never been able to decide if smoking is legal on New York subway platforms, but at that point I didn't care. I didn't care about anything except not having to look at the tracks again.

"It would have been different if it was murder," Sarah said. She sounded as if she'd convinced herself.

"It all happened so fast," Phoebe said. "First we were standing around talking about how no mugger was going to mess with a whole crowd of women, and then there was the train."

"Who's here from the police?" I asked her. "Could we get Martinez in on it?"

Phoebe looked confused. "He quit to go to law school," she said. "You know that."

"I forgot. What about Tony Marsh?"

This time she looked like she thought I was crazy. "Even if Tony were still a precinct cop, which he isn't, this would be the wrong precinct. Tony got promoted, don't you remember? He's a detective. With *Homicide?*"

"I know," I said.

"No, you don't know," she said. "I know. I was here."

"Homicide?" Sarah said.

"I don't mean I think it wasn't an accident," I said. "I mean, *look* at those people." I made a weak gesture in the direction of the knot of cops. "We don't know any of them. We won't be able to get them to tell us anything."

"That's true," Phoebe said. She shook her head. "It just doesn't matter. There isn't anything to tell. We were all a little drunk. We were standing on the edge of the platform. We were talking about—" She frowned. "No, we weren't. We weren't talking about muggers. We had been talking about muggers, but when the train came in, Verna was telling me about Ellery Queen."

"Ellery Queen."

"That Ellery Queen was a pseudonym. Or Ellery Queen was a lot of people, not one. Or something."

"Ellery Queen was the pseudonym of Frederic Dannay and Manfred B. Lee," I said.

"It didn't sound that simple," Phoebe said.

"I didn't hear anything about Ellery Queen," Sarah said. "I was talking to Miss Dooley about her paperweight."

Amelia pounded over to us, her face mottled gray and white, her nose red and on the verge of runny in the cold. New York subway stations are not well heated or well enclosed.

"Jesus Christ," she said. "Around and around and around. They never stop asking *questions.*"

"Questions about what?" I asked her.

Amelia gave me a look that was shrewd and unsubtle and contemptuous. "They want to know if she was a leaper," she said. "A leaper, for God's sake. What would make Verna leap in front of a train?"

I peered at her closely in the darkness. She was doing a good job of playing old shoot-from-the-hip Amelia, but in her eyes a hint of panic was struggling to break into terror.

"Verna was depressed at dinner," I said, considering suicide for the first time. "She kept talking about how badly her career was going."

"Horse manure," Amelia said, though I obviously hadn't made her feel any better. "Her career was in a slump. She wasn't about to starve to death."

"I was standing right next to her," Phoebe said. "I told you. She just *fell.*"

"Somebody's going to kill themselves over romantic suspense, it ought to be me," Amelia said. "Verna just had to write one of the things. I have to put out a whole line of them, one a month, under *my own name.*"

"Verna was using her own name," Phoebe said.

"*I'm* using my own name," Sarah said.

I squinted into the crowd near the tracks. "Did Marilou go home?" I asked. "I don't see her anywhere."

Amelia snorted. "Marilou's where you'd expect her to be. In the bathroom sucking up what she can and flushing the rest down a nice safe toilet. Now there's someone who ought to leap in front of a train over romantic suspense. She's got a contract to write one. She can't stay straight long enough to figure out what one *is.*"

"Marilou Saunders is going to write a romantic suspense?" I said. "Marilou Saunders can't *read.*"

Amelia adjusted her gown and the flaps of her stole. She had one of those fox stoles with the head and paws carefully preserved. A diamond and ruby dinner ring glittered in the light from the fluorescent over our heads.

"If the idiot police want to ask questions," Amelia said, "they ought to ask questions of *him.*" She made a dramatic sweep of the arm in the direction of Max Brady, no longer pugnacious and panicked in the middle of the platform. Max had wilted. He looked like a half-starved munchkin with encephalitis.

"Nobody knows what he's doing here," Amelia said. "Least of all him."

Nobody found out what Max was doing there, not that night. Phoebe remembered asking him to come on the round of bars because she "felt sorry for him and he looked lonely." Dana remembered sharing a cab with him. Caroline remembered De-Andrea getting disgusted and going home. We didn't have time to explore the issue. The police were interested in asking questions, but not in the middle of an empty subway station in the freezing late-October dawn. They started rounding us up for a trip to the precinct house. Nick got very lawyerly and advised us to go along.

"Actually," he told me when we were getting into a cab on Twenty-third Street (since we weren't material witnesses, the NYPD didn't think they owed us transportation), "I'd advise you to go home, but you wouldn't listen to me."

"No," I said. "I wouldn't."

"In that case, I'd advise you to keep your mouth shut. It's not a murder, Pay. It's a tragedy. It's a god-awful mess in more ways than one. It's not a murder."

"I didn't say anything about murder. I'm worried about Sarah."

"If the verdict is suicide, it'll be bad enough."

There were "Driver Allergic" signs all over the partition, but the driver was smoking a panatela, so I lit another cigarette and sat back in my seat. Nick had a very odd look on his face. His eyes were secretive. His mouth was tight.

"Why do I get this feeling you're not telling me something?" I asked him. "Why do I get this feeling something is going on I know nothing about?"

"I wouldn't know."

"Bullfeathers. You mentioned suicide. You were the second person to mention suicide."

"It's always a possibility. In cases like these."

"In cases like these."

"Exactly."

I took a deep drag. Every answer he gave wound him up tighter. He was no longer looking at me. He was staring out the window on his side of the cab, pretending an interest in the popcorn boxes in the gutters of Madison Avenue.

"Exactly nothing," I told him. "Something's been wrong all night. I can feel it. I didn't think anything of it before, but I think something of it now and it's not because Verna died. It's because you're acting weird, Nick. You aren't even talking like you."

He took a deep, going-on-the-offensive breath. "You've got murder on the brain," he said. "You've been involved in two cases and you see them behind every tree. If your grandmother died of heart failure, you'd go running to the dictionary of poisons to find out what drug could imitate coronary occlusion. It's become an obsession with you. There isn't any murder, McKenna."

"So there isn't any murder," I said. "If that's all you're worried about, don't worry about it. I told you I don't want to get involved in anything."

"I'll believe it when I see it."

"Believe it," I said. I was lying. I didn't care. I studied the tip of my cigarette, keeping my face turned away from him. "Why do you think Verna committed suicide? Why do the police think she did?"

"They try to keep it quiet, except for the insurance companies," Nick said. "For the sake of the family."

"Yes, yes," I said. "But why—"

"She was too far out on the tracks," Nick said. "Much too far out."

FIVE

"I was standing right *next* to her," Phoebe said. "First her *knees* buckled. Then she sort of fell *backward*. Then she pitched *forward*. Then she was sort of floating over the tracks."

The officer at the desk was middle-aged, middleweight, and overtired. His cheeks were jowly. The rings around his eyes were charcoal. He was wearing an expression of nearly inhuman patience.

"Let's try this again," he said. "First her knees bent. Then she pitched forward—"

"Backward," Phoebe said. "First her knees *buckled* and then she *fell* backward."

Caroline Dooley was sitting on a low plastic bench against the industrial green cement block wall, keeping her hands folded in her lap and her eyes closed. I sat down beside her, trying to decide what was going to make me feel worse: smoking with a policewoman glaring at me, or not smoking. I have been in a number of police stations. I haven't liked any of them. They're too crowded. Desks are pushed against each other and filing cabinets are shoved into every open space. They're also usually too noisy, but this was Gramercy Park at dawn. On the outside of the rail, Max Brady and the romantic suspense contingent milled around looking ready to collapse. On the other side, Phoebe harangued the officer, Nick held his head, and a sad-faced old lady sat in a far corner giving the details of a break-in to a very young patrolman at war with his typewriter.

"First her knees buckled," Phoebe said again.

I opted for the cigarette. "How long has this been going on?" I asked Caroline Dooley. I lit the cigarette with one of Phoebe's

Mamma Leone matches and put the spent match ostentatiously in the cuff of my pants.

Caroline didn't bother to open her eyes. "Forever," she said.

I tapped ash into my cupped hand. It hurt, but fortunately not for long.

"It's going to *keep* going on forever," Caroline said, "because Phoebe is sure of what she saw and the policeman is sure what happened and neither of them looks like the yielding type." She opened one eye at me. "You know Phoebe," she said.

I knew Phoebe. I also knew Caroline. Caroline's mind was a shrine to the *non sequitur.* If you asked her the time, you got the story of the Pink Panther umbrella she bought in the Village. If you were confused, she was offended. I was willing to bet I'd just heard the longest sane sentence she'd uttered since her First Communion Catechism class.

I took a very deep drag on my cigarette. I can outglare policewomen, but I don't like to do it more than I have to.

"What I can't understand," I told Caroline, "is what you people were doing in a subway station at five o'clock in the morning. Any subway station, never mind *that* subway station. What are we doing in Gramercy Park?"

"Oh, *God.*" Caroline sat up straight, making a valiant but doomed effort to look alert. Caroline was always trying to look alert. And on top of things.

"Well," she said. "There was Miss English. Miss English is going to be a great romantic suspense writer."

"Right," I said.

"Somebody had never been on a subway train," Caroline said.

"You must have been plastered," I said.

"I am never plastered," Caroline said. "Phoebe was plastered. *Amelia* was plastered. Marilou—"

We both looked across the room at Marilou. A patrolman had stationed himself less than half a foot from her seat and was glaring down at her. From the way Marilou was grinning, both Caroline and I knew she didn't have a thing on her. The patrolman knew it, too. It was driving him crazy.

Caroline stared at the ceiling. "First we went to the Mudd

Club," she said, "then we went walking, and we walked and walked. You wouldn't believe the kind of people out on the streets of New York at this time of night. Then Verna put the heel of her shoe into Mr. Brady's ankle. Then—" Caroline frowned. "*Verna* was plastered. In fact, I think that's the first time I ever saw Verna plastered. She kept talking to herself."

"About what?"

"People don't talk to themselves *about* anything," Caroline said. "They talk to themselves. If they had something to talk *about*, they'd talk to someone else."

"Oh," I said.

"She kept babbling about mistakes and all the ones anybody ever made and men and it was all their fault and damn her ex-husband anyway." Caroline looked sideways at me. "You ever met Verna's ex-husband?"

"No," I said. "Somebody told me he was a psychiatrist."

"He has a therapy group for the husbands of romance writers. Helping them cope with their wives' success."

I needed another cigarette.

"It's very necessary work," Caroline said. I couldn't decide if she sounded defensive or smug. "You wouldn't believe the kind of neuroses these men get."

"Verna," I said desperately. "Verna was drunk."

"Oh, God," Caroline said. "I'd hate to be an agent. Dana must be a *saint.*"

"Right," I said again.

"Dana got her by the arm," Caroline said. "Verna, I mean. They started talking about—mystery stories. Agatha Christie. Ellery Queen. Somebody. Then Miss English said she'd never been in a subway, so Phoebe started herding us up to Twenty-third Street—"

"From the Mudd Club?" I asked, trying to hold onto sanity.

"Never go near Bellevue at night," Caroline said. "They let these people out and even the people know they shouldn't be out and they come back asking to be let in but the gates are locked and—"

"The Mudd Club," I said. "*The Mudd Club.*"

"Oh," Caroline said. "We were above Eighteenth already. It was a long walk."

"I can see that."

"*Anyway,* Max Brady got hold of Verna then and started trying to loan her a copy of *The Big Sleep.* Which is what she was doing the last time I saw her before the train." The train seemed to get through something heavy and thick in Caroline's brain. "My God," she said. "What a *mess.*"

I put my cigarette out under my heel, picked the butt off the floor, and put it in my pants cuff with the match. Then I folded my legs up under me and lit another cigarette.

"I can't understand how you ended up with Max Brady in the first place," I said.

"Neither can I," Caroline said. "First he was there, then he wasn't there, then he was there again."

"What?"

"He was with us at Eddie Condon's. Then he disappeared. Then he reappeared at the Mudd Club. I think."

"How did he find you at the Mudd Club?"

"How am I supposed to know?"

I thought of saying "You were there," but I didn't. It would have been useless.

Nick leaned over the dividing rail and waved frantically in my direction.

"Could you come here?" he asked me. "We want you to talk to Phoebe."

The scene was frozen in amber, written as history, decided for all time. Phoebe had her arms crossed over her chest and her eyebrows lowered. Her cheeks looked hollow, meaning she was probably biting them from the inside. The policeman was red where he wasn't black and blue and looked a breath away from going for his gun.

"Let me bring you up to date," he said.

"Let *me* bring you up to date," Phoebe said. She turned to the policeman. "Patience *knows* me. I'm not stupid and I'm not blind and I've *never* been a liar."

"Gotcha," the policeman said. He looked her up and down, checking out the floor-length royal blue velvet caftan, the eight strands of rope diamonds, the sixteen diamond and sapphire rings, the pear-shaped diamond earrings so heavy they made her earlobes droop. I could almost hear what he was thinking: this woman might or might not be a liar, but she was certainly a nut. He held out his hand to me. "I'm Jerry O'Reilly," he said.

"Pay McKenna," I said. I found a chair, dragged it over, and sat down in it. Phoebe has a lot of staying power.

"The problem we have here," Jerry O'Reilly said, "is I think your friend is mistaken. She says—"

"Patience knows what I've been saying," Phoebe said. "Everybody knows what I've been saying. They heard me in *Hoboken.*"

"Gotcha," Jerry O'Reilly said. "The thing is, this Miss Train couldn't have fallen backward like you said and then pitched forward. Nobody could do that unless they were pushed, and you say—"

"Patience," Phoebe turned her chair to face me. "I was standing right next to her. I was looking behind her trying to see up the tracks if the train was coming."

"She was that close to the edge?" I said. "She was so close you looked behind her and saw the train coming?"

"I didn't see anything," Phoebe said. "I looked to see. I'm short. I spend a lot of time trying to look around other people to see what's going on. I was looking past her back and nobody put a hand on her back."

"It's a question of physics," Jerry O'Reilly said in exasperation. "Maybe her knees buckled and she fell backward, but if she pitched forward after that, somebody had to be pushing her."

"Maybe she swayed," I suggested.

"She didn't sway," Phoebe said. "She fell, and her knees sort of collapsed. She almost fell into whoever was behind her, I don't remember who. And nobody put a hand on her back and pushed her."

"You stand up and try it," Jerry O'Reilly said. "You just stand right up and *try* it."

Phoebe ignored him. "We went into the subway station and we

were a little nervous," she said. "We were standing in a knot, sort of, huddled up for protection. We were talking about muggers and spooking ourselves and we kept getting closer to each other just in case. I wasn't just standing next to her, I was almost leaning against her."

"He says you can talk some sense into her," Jerry O'Reilly said, shooting his head to the side so that it pointed at Nick's nose. "What about it?"

I contemplated my cigarette. I contemplated my nose. I contemplated what Nick was going to say when he heard what I had to say. Then I told the truth.

"If Phoebe says that's what she saw," I said, "that's what she saw. If Phoebe says that's what she saw, that's probably what *happened.*"

"Jesus *Christ,*" Nick said.

"I told you," Phoebe said.

"Make it murder," Jerry O'Reilly said. "I'll listen to a murder. I won't listen to a suspension of the laws of gravity."

"I'll explain it again from the beginning," Phoebe said.

Jerry O'Reilly wasn't having any. "Go home," he said. "Levitate. Do whatever it is you do when you're alone. I don't care."

"I'm just trying," Phoebe started.

"I'm trying to take statements from witnesses who make sense," Jerry O'Reilly said. "Someone will type this crap up for you. You can come down tomorrow and sign it. Get *out* of here."

Phoebe shrugged and started gathering up her string bag and evening wrap. Romance writers are the only women in America who still buy real 1950s-style date-dress evening wraps. O'Reilly shouted "Dooley" over our heads. Phoebe looked at him and frowned.

"I'm really not trying to be obstructionist," she said. "I just saw what I saw."

"That's all right." I patted her head. Everyone ends up patting Phoebe's head. She's so small and compact. "You go home," I told her. "I'll sit around and wait for Sarah."

"I'll sit around and wait for Sarah," Nick said—generously, in this case, because he wasn't very pleased with either of us. "I have to stay here for Amelia and Caroline anyway. I'll bring Sarah home when she's made her statement."

"I might as well stick around," I said. "I'm not going to get any sleep."

"Cancel your appointments," Nick said. He looked worried. It is his contention that I do not eat, sleep, or relax anywhere near enough to keep me healthy.

I made a vague gesture at the wall clock. "It's quarter after seven and I'm due for a session at Images in less than two hours."

"PR?" Phoebe asked sympathetically.

"Last time I was on television, I looked fuzzy," I said. "According to my lady at Doubleday anyway." I yawned.

Caroline Dooley's voice floated up from the far side of the room, squeaky and nervous.

"The thing is, Officer, if I had to reconstruct the scene as I saw it, you see, I think I'd have to agree with Miss Damereaux about the sequence and—"

Sarah was waiting for us at the rail. Her eyes were shining. Her squeamishness had been washed away by excitement.

"Oh," she said, breathless and agitated. "It *is* going to be a murder. It *is.*"

SIX

I did not do well at Images. They knew what I *ought* to look like. I knew what I *did* look like. There was no possible compromise. I have strong bones and wide eyes and high cheekbones. I could be the illegitimate child of John Lindsay and a full-blooded Cherokee. They thought I ought to look like Cheryl Tiegs. Or Christie Brinkley. Or Farrah Fawcett. I got out of there at quarter to twelve, nearly crazy from lack of sleep and more than murderous from arguing. I didn't care how fuzzy I looked on television. I had no intention of turning into another cookie cutter imitation of every other blond WASP on the celebrity circuit. Images wanted to give me something called a "California cut." The only thing I like that uses "California" as an adjective is avocados.

I turned down Fifth Avenue, trying to decide what I thought of what had happened to Verna Train. I know people who can party till dawn, come home, take a shower, and show up at the office two hours later looking like they just returned from a vacation in Bali. I am not one of them. On seven hours' sleep I am awake. On six, I am operative. Less than six leaves me temporarily stupid and emotionally schizophrenic.

I hadn't known Verna Train. I knew things about her—she was divorced; she wrote moderately successful contemporary romances; she was capable of physical aggression when angry or drunk or both. What I had was like a description under "Cast of Characters" at the beginning of a script. It was only a stencil. The stencil didn't say anything to me. She had been unkind to Sarah. I hadn't liked it.

I liked the way I was thinking even less. Nick had reason for his suspicions. I do tend to see murder—cold, deliberate, and brutal—behind everything these days. Worse, I never escape from it. In the past two years I have spent all my time either involved in murders or writing about them. When I return from vacations, my mailbox is full of fan letters enclosing "something extra." In the past six months, I have received a complete set of press clippings on the DeQuincy, Iowa, disembowelment murders; four sharp knives; a photo essay (amateur—Kodak snapshots pasted to typing paper) on an autopsy; and a detailed plan for the assassination of Claude Rains, who is already dead. That was what I was getting *before* the book came out, when I was just a picture and a name in newspaper stories. Once the book came out, I stopped opening fan mail, got a telephone number so unlisted even AT&T doesn't know what it is, and started handing over any packages left on my doorstep to the bomb squad.

Every time I thought about Verna Train dying, something inside me wanted it to be murder. I was not *entirely* unreasonable. Facts, after all, were facts. If Phoebe hadn't been so sure of what she'd seen in the subway station, I might have talked myself into believing a verdict of accidental death before I got five blocks downtown. Phoebe, however, was sure. Phoebe sees what she sees when she sees it. In a room full of distracted witnesses, Phoebe will be the one person with an accurate account of whatever happened. This is true even when Phoebe is drunk. She is more tenaciously connected to the world than the rest of us.

I could not think of a single reason why anyone would want to murder Verna Train. Most murders are committed for money. Verna Train did not have real money. She did not have lasting fame, which meant she was worth more alive than dead to both her agent and her publisher. Someone with Phoebe's or Amelia's followings might generate enough ink in dying to sell a few books on her coffin, but for someone like Verna to get that kind of press, she would have to die spectacularly. Falling under a subway train would not be enough.

Which left me where I had started—with Verna dead, possibly (probably) from suicide or subway accident. There might be hidden motives—I'd known a few—but Verna was not well placed enough for any of the ones I could think of. The woman had had a minor career that looked on the way to a prolonged downswing when she died. She hadn't had any clout.

I hadn't had any sleep. I stopped in the middle of a block, trying to make the dizziness go away and counting the hours since I'd had anything to eat. When I have gone without sleep, I lose my appetite. Since my body has almost no fat to draw on (I often think it does, but it doesn't), the result is light-headedness, nausea, and a tendency to giggle. I was at Sixtieth Street. I had a distinct memory of a Hamburger Heaven at Fifty-seventh and Lexington. Hamburger Heavens make Roquefort cheeseburgers. I *deserved* a Roquefort cheeseburger.

I was halfway down the long avenue block between Fifth and Madison when I saw the bookstore. I saw it out of the corner of my eye. I was thinking about Verna. I felt the odd wrench in my stomach and the sudden tightening of my nerves, but I didn't realize what was wrong until I'd passed the display window.

What was wrong was *me*. I backed up. There was a pyramid of books in the window, one of those ten-foot-high house-of-cards constructions revolving on a turntable. The largest part of the pyramid was taken up by copies of the new Judith Krantz. The second largest part was taken up by copies of the new V. C. Andrews. The tenth largest part was taken up by me. What I had seen was the black-and-white studio portrait Doubleday had commissioned for the back of my book, visible when the turntable presented its backside to the street.

This happened every fifteen seconds. It was like having my name in blinking neon lights.

I am not one of those writers who pretend to hate publicity. I want all the publicity I can get. I want to spend fifty weeks at the top of the New York *Times* bestseller list. I put up with Marilou Saunders to get on her talk show. I thank critics for bad reviews —if I happen to meet them at the kind of party where we are both expected to be civilized. I was not, however, ready for that window.

I paced back and forth in front of it, trying to decide what to think of it. I wondered how anyone ever got a book off a display like that. I considered the possibility that this bookstore didn't sell books. It ordered books to make displays of, giving its over-sensitive homosexual millionaire owners a chance to Show What They Could Do with Design. I felt dizzy again. I decided to go in.

There was a long, low table of books behind the revolving turntable. On that table were Judith Krantz's book, and V. C. Andrews' book, and mine. I picked up one of mine and turned it over and over in my hands. It was thick and heavy and felt good —about the weight of a doorstop, which is what most critics use books for. The studio portrait was also good. It looked like me. It didn't look like a studio portrait.

I put the book back on the table. It looked very credible sitting there among all the other books. It looked like a real book.

I had actually written a real book.

Somebody had actually published the real book I had written. In hardcover.

To be sold in bookstores.

Good *lord.*

I was telling myself that panicking over good news was the mark of a lunatic when someone tapped the arm of my jacket and "ahemmed" politely in my ear.

"That's a *very* good book," the little voice said. "Very scary."

I turned around. The girl standing behind me had her hands clasped at her belt and her face tortured into an expression of extravagantly expectant helpfulness. She was pale and wan and plain. Her hair (dull brown, wiry) was a mess. One look in her eyes and you knew she *hated* working in that store.

She peered at me through heavy horn-rimmed glasses.

"Miss *McKenna,*" she said. "My *goodness.*"

Nobody in New York says "My goodness." Nobody wears four-inch horn-rims either, but there we were. This girl's horn-rims were purely ornamental. There was no magnification in the glass.

I gave her the best smile I could manage with a head full of sleepless confusion and said, "I've never seen it in a bookstore before. Then I saw it in the window, and—"

"I just read it," the girl said. "It was wonderful." Her voice was very firm. I wondered if it would be as firm if she were talking to V. C. Andrews. V. C. Andrews doesn't know the difference between the English language and a banana split.

The girl was kneeling on the avocado green carpet, pulling copies of my book from the drawer in the side of the display table.

"If you have a minute, it would really help if you signed some of these," she said. "In this neighborhood they like them signed if we can get them signed. We have signed copies of the Krantz book, of course, because we always have signed copies of the Krantz book, we always give her a party, but if you have a minute—"

She thrust ten copies of my book into my arms. She picked up twice that many for herself.

"If you sign them on the title page," she said, "we can't return them. It's as good as a sale." She grinned.

I grinned back. "Why doesn't PR tell me these things?"

"Oh," she waved a hand in the air. *"PR."*

I know an ally when I see one. I hooked the books under my arms. "If you've got a place for me to sit," I said.

She was already halfway across the carpet to the back of the store. "We have a little office," she said. "I can give you some coffee. All you have to do is sign your name. Then when people come in asking for them inscribed"—she made the word sound like bad Park Avenue French for something unprintable—"I can give them some of these." She pushed open a heavy metal door and held it until I walked through. "Anybody stupid enough to pay half a million dollars for a one-bedroom apartment," she said, "is stupid enough to feel superior about a signature."

The office was small and cramped and functional, with a rickety little desk and a minuscule chair wedged between unsteady piles of books. At least half the books were paperbacks. At least 90 percent of the paperbacks were romances. There was an overflowing green tin ashtray on a bookshelf above my head. I took it down, lit a cigarette, and dropped the match among the butts.

"Just your name," the girl said again. "If it was before publication, I'd have you date them, but that's the only kind of date these people want. Like other people will see the book on the coffee table and pick it up and read the date and think the guy who owns it has some kind of in."

"I could always backdate it," I said.

"Whatever for?"

"It would be nice if you actually sold some of these things. I'd like to be read, for God's sake."

The girl dismissed this with another wave. "These people don't read," she said. "I mean, they do, but they read trashy paperback originals. I mean, I like trashy paperback originals. Even so. These people pick up three impressive-looking hardcovers and a dozen Phoebe Damereaux and pretend the Damereaux are for their invalid mothers. If you know what I mean."

"I know Phoebe Damereaux," I said. "Long may she wave."

"Yeah," the girl admitted. "She's pretty good. And she's in hardcover now, so I suppose she doesn't count. But you see what I'm saying."

I said I did and started signing books. I was very tired. My signature looked like a secret code for the mining of Haiphong Harbor. In Vietnamese.

"What I heard," I told her, "is nobody's reading romance novels any more."

"Nobody's reading the lines," she nodded emphatically, making a wild gesture at the towers of paperbacks surrounding us. "Look at these returns. God, you should see the kind of trouble we have with those. Sabotage. I'm not kidding."

"Sabotage?"

"With the dumps. You know, the display things. People come in and destroy other people's dumps, or move them, or hide them. And then there's Harlequin. They want to opt out of the romance book centers and have us carry only Harlequin, which is ridiculous because Harlequin doesn't sell as well among the yuppies as some of the others, and what we have here is a yuppie market. Then everybody is buying everybody else out, and lines are folding right and left, and God knows what all. It's a mess."

I took a deep drag on my cigarette. My signature was beginning to look like a biology class drawing of a frog.

"What about the contemporaries?" I asked her. "You know a writer named Verna Train?"

That took her a while. She seemed to be communing with a central book file located somewhere in her cerebellum.

"Verna Train," she said finally. "Charla Menlowe."

"What?"

"It's like a clump," she said. "Like actresses. Brooke Adams and Karen Allen are a clump. They look alike. They take the same kinds of parts. You see? Verna Train and Charla Menlowe are a clump, they do the same stuff. They're good enough to have an audience, but they're nothing special. But people recognize the names, you see, because they were all over the place during the boom, so if they did something else, we'd want to handle it, we'd make some money just from the name recognition. But not their romance stuff. Not anymore."

"Right," I said. I knew all this already.

"In fact," she said, "that's what's happening. There's a brand-new line coming out in a few months taking all these sorts of middle-level people and putting them into romantic suspense. We're very excited about it. Not that we're excited about romantic suspense—that's not going to go anywhere. But the recognition factor, that's something else. You know about romantic suspense?"

I knew more than I wanted to know about romantic suspense. I knew more than she knew about the line she was describing. I was glad she thought it would be successful, especially since Nick didn't. I bent over the fifteenth book and forced the pen to make a signature. It looked vaguely like a crossword puzzle grid.

"You know," she said. "All that infighting doesn't help. The kind of readers who buy the line stuff don't want to think of their favorite writers as—as bitches."

"The genre is doomed," I told her.

"Probably," she said. "But some of these women are monsters, believe me. And it gets in the papers, and it gets around. Take that Amelia Samson. There's this story going around, it was in *Romantic Times,* that when Miss Train started losing sales and her publisher wanted to drop her, Miss Samson could have stopped them but she refused. And they've known each other forever. They're supposed to be friends. Some people say Miss Samson even did a little pushing to get Miss Train ousted. What respectable yuppie wants to be associated with a person like that?"

All the respectable yuppies I knew *behaved* like that, but I didn't say so. I didn't say the story didn't sound like Amelia, although it didn't. "I don't suppose it's hurt Amelia any," I told her.

The little girl shook her head emphatically. "It's hurt Amelia Samson a lot. That and the fact that she's still living in 1921. But believe me, that sort of nonsense doesn't do anyone any good."

My signature now looked like a route map for the N train.

It was time to quit.

SEVEN

It was the beginning of the lunch rush, one of those times when the streets of New York are crowded with cars and people frozen into immobility and distinctly unhappy about it. Even if I could have found a cab, I wouldn't have been able to get anywhere in it. I would just have traded crowd claustrophobia for traffic jam. I started downtown on foot, dodging arm-swinging secretaries in pastel linen skirts and ankle-strap shoes, ignoring "Walk" and "Don't Walk" signs. "Walk" and "Don't Walk" signs don't mean anything on Lexington Avenue at half past twelve. Crowds form an unbroken stream. In the restaurants, they form the breathing equivalent of an unsplittable atom. I took a look into Hamburger Heaven. Even if I could fight my way to the counter, I'd never carve out enough room to eat. I let three girls in dirndl minidresses and Art Deco legwarmers push past me and took comfort in the fact that Dana never ate lunch. If Dana ever started eating lunch, her wardrobe would become inoperative.

I turned south and west, running a little to keep myself awake. It got the adrenaline flowing, but it didn't clear my head.

In the lobby of Dana's building, the stream was running against me. Assistant art directors in black tights and black turtlenecks and rose jumpers, assistant personnel directors in navy blue wool and frilly white blouses, assistant editors in tweed skirts and "good" (single-ply) cashmere sweaters and last year's slingbacks—all of them were on their way out of the elevators and into the street. I ducked through the nearest pair of air-lock doors, realized I was in a "30th Floor Only" car, and ducked out again. I waited by a set of doors with a sign on them saying "22–49," flattened myself against the wall to let the horde disgorge, then darted in to push the button for "26." At certain times of day, finding the right elevator going in the right direction in a New York office building can be the emotional equivalent of storming the beach at Iwo Jima.

The twenty-sixth floor was one of the reasons I'd hired Dana. Most agents work out of their apartments, or rent two- or three-room suites in modest little buildings in the Forties. Dana had the entire floor. She had three telephone banks. She had wall-to-wall Bigelows on the floor and framed publicity posters for half a dozen bestsellers on her walls. The bestsellers were a little dated —Dana used to specialize in mainstream fiction, which has been losing out to the genres and the nonfiction how-to books *(Fifteen Minutes to Thinner Thighs and Your First Million)*—but they were very famous. Some of them were famous enough to have made six-figure movie deals before anybody had ever heard of six-figure movie deals.

I rapped my knuckles against the receptionist's desk, smiled a greeting, and took a very full, very black cup of coffee from the blue plastic Dripmaster on the end table next to the John Homans couch. I looked at the little plastic dish of rat pellets on the floor in the corner and wondered if there was anywhere in New York without a rodent problem (cockroaches are not a problem; cockroaches are an Alternative Population). I swallowed the coffee in one long chug and headed for Dana's office. The receptionist would buzz me through, but I wasn't worried about interrupting anything. Dana does not see people in her office during lunch. Dana sees them on the phone during lunch.

She was getting off the phone as I walked in.

"You wouldn't believe who that was," she said. "You wouldn't believe *what* that was."

"Haven't had any sleep either, I take it." I dropped into a chair and started searching for cigarettes.

"That was some idiot in PR over at Gallard Rowson," Dana said. "She's got an idea to promote Verna's book. She wants to put Verna's bio on the back cover and start the text with"—Dana paused dramatically—"'She lived dangerously and died violently, but before she did, she left us this book.'"

"Well," I said. "The syntax is interesting."

"Oh, come now," Dana said. "Doubleday can't be that bad."

"Doubleday isn't bad at all," I said. "It's PR. PR people aren't Doubleday, or Dortman & Hodges, or Avon, or Austin, Stoddard & Trapp. PR people are PR people. They have schools for them."

"I suppose they must," Dana said.

I found my cigarettes wedged into the envelope of my American Express bill. I extracted them. Dana was fussing with papers on her desk, looking for something that wasn't there. I found a pack of Monk's Inn matches, lit up, and threw the spent match and a handful of scrap paper into Dana's Steuben glass ashtray.

"I thought you were bringing Sarah English with you," she muttered. "Now what the hell—" She brushed her short, Vidal Sassooned hair out of her eyes. "I've lost the specs, of course. I'll have Fanny bring in another set." She buzzed through on her desk phone. "You've got to tell Miss English to come in and talk to Jane Herman. As long as she's in the city, we might as well get things straightened out."

"Jane Herman?"

Dana sighed impatiently. "Jane sold Miss English's book. I don't read unsolicited mail anymore. Even recommended unsolicited mail." Her mouth twisted wryly. "Maybe I should start. That was the best romantic suspense this office has seen yet, and Jane didn't have the sense to submit it to our line. She just shot it straight off to Austin, Stoddard & Trapp. Without even telling me."

"I thought your line had to have brand-name authors."

"And celebrities," Dana said. "Yes, it does. Gallard Rowson took one look at the competition and insisted on a hook. Assholes."

"Right," I said.

"Not that it wasn't a good idea," Dana said again. "It was a great idea. You should see the orders. You should see the subscriptions. Subscriptions are sales. The readers want celebrities."

"Figures," I said.

Dana took a pile of proofs out of a drawer and tossed them to me. *Passionate Intrigues* was written in red and black script across the top of each cover. The cover paintings bled into the spines. The one for *Mysteries of the Heart* showed a man and a woman, locked in lecherous embrace, dangling from a rope suspended from the bottom of a glider descending into the Grand Canyon at dusk. The man had his lips as close to the woman's nipple as genre romance covers will allow, which meant he was half a breath from swallowing it. The woman was wearing an off-the-shoulder peasant blouse and four-inch high-heeled sandals.

"The competition is awful," Dana said. "Judy Sullivan over at Walker. Bernstein and Marcel—you know Bernstein and Marcel? They're general agents, but they somehow managed to sew up half the decent mystery writers in the world, it seems like, and most of romance. They're packaging for Avon and they've got *everybody.*"

"You've got Verna Train," I said.

"Oh yes," Dana said. "I've got Ivy Samuels Tree and Hazel Ganz writing as Harriet Lowry and God knows who else. I've got the names; I'm just not sure I've got the quality. What does Hazel know about romantic suspense?" She tapped her teeth with the tip of her silver Tiffany T-pen. Then she put the pen in her pocket. She was careful to position the T-shaped clip exactly in the center of the linen flap. "You wouldn't want to try romantic suspense?" she suggested. "I could pry your Jeri Andrews pseudonym out of Farret."

"Jeri Andrews has retired," I said.

"I was afraid of that." There was a knock on the door. Dana called "Come in" and sat looking regal while a thin, pimply-faced secretary scurried to the desk with a sheaf of photocopies in a blue plastic folder. "Excellent," Dana said. "You can go to lunch now."

The secretary did everything but kiss her feet. Dana tossed the photocopies to me.

"Look them over," she said, "but a quarter of a million on signing is a quarter of a million on signing. Plus residuals. As long as you deal with network programming, you're dealing with business people. The movie people think they're one up on God and they rob you blind. And you can't prove it."

"Double cost accounting," I said wisely.

"People should stop teaching you buzz words."

I threw the folder onto her desk. "Okay," I said. "I'm not crazy. It's a big, unusual deal and you're a brilliant agent and with 15 percent of this you can afford to take me to Lutèce for dinner. How's that?"

"Images called," Dana said.

I sighed. "I tried," I said. "I really did. But I haven't had any sleep and I look lousy in the Images style and I don't understand if I have to go on television why I can't just—"

"You can't," Dana said. "I told you when we started. If you want to go this route, you have to keep in shape, you have to look the part, you have to play by the rules. If you want to be famous, McKenna, you have to look famous."

"Everybody famous has to look like everybody else famous?"

"Maybe Images was the wrong place," Dana said. "But we've tried you with Estée Lauder and Merle Norman and Elizabeth Arden and even Mary Kay, for God's sake. You managed to get yourself thrown out of Mary Kay."

"I've got to go over to AST," I said, getting into my jacket. "Someone in PR wants to talk promotion on the paper."

The buzzer went off on Dana's desk. She picked up the receiver, listened for a minute, then hung up. "Damn Phoebe Damereaux," she said. "There's a cop in Reception waiting to talk to me."

Radd Stassen was not a cop. He was, as he put it, "a private." The challenge was to discover a private what. Radd Stassen had thirty-two expensively capped teeth, tinted contact lenses that made his eyes look rabbit pink, and tiny embroidered emblems sewn onto all his clothes. His hair was slicked back and sleek, like a lounge lizard's in a silent movie. He bounced on the balls of his feet, trying to give an impression of energy.

He was carrying an outsized manila envelope. He patted it fondly, sat down without waiting to be asked, and crossed his legs at the knees.

"I represent Jane Minetti Brady," he said. "We're going to call you as a witness in a civil suit."

On the other side of the desk, Dana shifted in her chair, frowned, tapped her forehead. She didn't know what was in her office, which meant she couldn't decide if I should be there.

Radd Stassen decided for her. He put his face very close to mine, squinted, and nodded emphatically. "The blonde," he said. "I've got notes about a blonde." He took an untidy mess of papers from the manila envelope and shuffled through them. "Pat Campbell," he said.

"Patience," I said. "Patience Campbell McKenna."

"Same thing," he said.

I did not know what to do with someone who thought "Pat Campbell" and "Patience Campbell McKenna" were the same thing. I hunkered down into my coat, warding off the cold that was more a function of fatigue than room temperature. I was falling asleep. If Dana and Radd Stassen got into something surreal, I could pass out in my chair.

One look at Dana's face should have told me that no matter how surrealistic Radd Stassen might be as a person, his mission was anything but. She was suddenly very alert, erect and rigid in her swivel chair, eyes forward, frown plastered from one side of her jaw to the other. She looked the way she looks when someone mentions money in contract negotiations.

"I haven't come for information," Radd Stassen said. "We've got information."

"What have you come for?" Dana asked him. "Doughnuts?"

Radd Stassen smiled. It amounted to a neck-tightening grimace and a shimmer of teeth.

"We already know you act as agent for Maxwell Arthur Brady," he said.

"Bob Brown acts as agent for Maxwell Arthur Brady," Dana said. "Would you like his number?"

"You act as agent for Maxwell Arthur Brady writing as"— Radd Stassen checked his papers—"Melissa Crowell." He put the papers on his knees and patted the edges of the stack, pretending to straighten them. "It's in your capacity as agent for Maxwell Arthur Brady writing as Melissa Crowell that we're going to call you in the civil suit. Jane Minetti Brady has a certain amount of interest in Maxwell Arthur Brady writing as Melissa Crowell."

I woke up long enough to get a cigarette out of the pack in my jacket pocket and (almost) unravel Radd Stassen's show-and-tell.

"Melissa Crowell," I said. "Melissa Crowell writes bodice rippers. You mean Max Brady is Melissa Crowell?"

"Exactly," Radd Stassen said.

"Ridiculous," Dana said.

"You take a rape prevention class at the New School Monday and Thursday nights at seven-thirty," Radd Stassen said. "Maxwell Arthur Brady teaches a class on the history of the private detective at the New School Monday and Thursday nights at seven."

"I take a rape class at the New School," Dana said.

"We know that's where you're passing business information," Radd Stassen said. "Outside the men's room on the third floor. We've got witnesses."

"Bull manure," Dana said.

"Jane Minetti Brady got a divorce from Maxwell Arthur Brady in 1969," Radd Stassen said. "It's a percentage of income, which translates into a percentage of *known* income. We now know about this income."

Dana sighed, elaborately, grotesquely, exaggeratedly. It was such an out-of-character sound for her, I woke up again. I had a sudden vision of a class called "Acting for Agents," held in a fifth-floor Chelsea loft every Monday and Wednesday lunch and run by a ringer from William Morris. If it didn't exist, it ought to.

"Mr. Stetson—" Dana started.

"Stassen," Radd Stassen smiled energetically. "Raddford Hugh Stassen. Know what's great about my name? It's my name. The one I was born with."

"It must have been quite a trial in Little League," Dana said.

"About Maxwell Arthur Brady writing as Melissa Crowell," Radd Stassen said.

The buzzer went off on Dana's desk. She picked up her phone, listened with impatience, and said, "That's all right. Go to lunch

. . . no, go to lunch now. I'll come out and get it." She replaced the phone. "If you'll excuse me. This is *very* important and I've been *waiting* all *morning.*"

She got up and headed for the door, heels sinking into the carpet, hands rigidly at her sides. Radd and I watched her go. She had more self-control than either of us. She left that office as if she were leaving an empty space.

She shut the door with a snap. Radd rearranged his big, intrusive body in his chair, wiggled his foot (the one in the air), and smiled at me.

"Going to call her lawyer," he said. "They always do."

I started hunting for another cigarette. "Somebody buzzed her," I said.

"Somebody buzzed her to say they were going to lunch," Radd Stassen said. "It's an excuse. She did this Maxwell Arthur Brady a favor, now she wants to know what her liability is. She'll come back, deny everything, then come into court and change her story under oath. They do it every time."

"I didn't even know Max used to be married," I said.

"Ancient history," Radd Stassen said.

I found the cigarette. I found the matches. I found a three-week overdue electric bill. "Lisa," I said. "All the time I've known him, he's been going out with a girl named Lisa." I thought about it. "Never seen her," I said.

"The redhead," Radd Stassen said. "That's recent. Last year, year and a half. Before that there was—" He consulted his papers. Every time he consulted his papers, he had to look through the stack page by page. He had apparently yet to hear about categorization by subject. Or even alphabetization. "The older woman," he muttered. He seized a page. "Train," he said. "Mrs. Verna Train."

I burned my fingers with the match. "Are you *nuts?*"

"Of course I'm not nuts. I've got pictures." He was offended.

"They hated each other," I told him. "They did physical violence to each other."

"Lately. Before Lisa, they used to do other things to each

other." Radd smiled. I was getting very tired of his smile. "Mrs. Brady has kept an eye on Mr. Brady since the divorce," he said.

"Mrs. Brady must be better than the KGB."

"This Train got him started on the romance stuff."

I lit another match and applied it very carefully to my cigarette. Verna Train, in a snit over Max Brady's affair with the redheaded Lisa, threatens to tell Max's ex-wife that Max is making a lot of money hacking out bodice rippers under a pseudonym. Max Brady therefore kills Verna Train before she can talk. Possible.

"Tell me," I said. "Was it Verna who told you Max was Melissa Crowell?"

"I can't tell you where I got my information." He looked shocked.

He shouldn't have given me the information, but it seemed ungrateful to say so. Instead, I tried nodding sympathetically. "Of course not," I told him.

Radd Stassen expanded. "People read these private-eye novels and don't realize what it's like," he said. "The name of this game is money. You want to make a lot of money, you got to protect your contacts."

"Of course."

"What I do, it's a lot like what a cop does. Except cops can't afford a night out at the Hudson Bay Inn." He coughed into his hand. "You like the Hudson Bay Inn?"

"Um," I said.

"You like Oriental sexual positions? That's my hobby, Oriental sexual positions."

I had let my eyes close again. Now I opened them—for a good look at Radd Stassen. He was starring in his own movie. His part was being played by Burt Reynolds.

"What I am, you know, I'm one of these guys who like to get around."

"Right," I said.

"I like to get a lot of experience. Try new things. Blow off a little steam."

"Right," I said again.

"I see a lot of interesting stuff in my work. I stay in shape. I run in the park every morning. I get out every night. I figure, if you don't burn the candle at both ends, what's the candle got two ends *for?*"

It was time to put a stop to this. "Actually," I said. "I'm not so fond of the Hudson Bay Inn. I sort of prefer the Four Seasons."

The Four Seasons is one of those restaurants where dinner for two can run two hundred dollars without wine. Radd Stassen went *white*.

He was saved by Dana, bustling through the door with a pile of folders in her hands and a little too much color in her cheeks.

"Idiots," she was saying. "Ask them for projections and you get—" She noticed Radd Stassen. "Oh," she said. "You're still here."

Radd Stassen started pawing through his pile of papers. "I've got some documents," he said.

I got out of my chair. I might be "the blonde," but that could mean anything. Radd Stassen had no right to keep me in Dana's office. With any luck, Dana wouldn't want to keep me in her office either.

"I'm very tired," I said. "I think I'll cancel my appointment at AST and go home to sleep."

Dana frowned. "Don't cancel any appointments," she said. "Especially any appointments about promotion."

"You want I should faint while trying to make up my mind between poster proposals?"

"I *want*," Dana started.

Radd Stassen interrupted her. "I want to talk to you about this Englishwoman," he said. "Was he leaving this redhead for this Englishwoman? What's her name?"

"What are you talking about?" I said.

Radd Stassen waved his papers in triumph. "We've got pictures," he said. "Last night. He was all over her."

EIGHT

I got out of there. It took a pretense of idiocy. It took putting out my cigarette before I was finished with it. I didn't care. I was glad to know Radd Stassen wasn't much of a private detective (an *Englishwoman*, for God's sake) and glad to be making my escape.

Radd Stassen had given me a motive for the murder of Verna Train, if Verna had been murdered. In fact, he had almost given me two. Almost but not quite. I tried to envision Jane Minetti Brady following Max through a succession of jazz bars and campy pickup joints and finally pushing Verna off a subway platform in frustration. It didn't work. It was Jane Minetti Brady's hired detectives who were following Max. She might have been along for the ride, but I couldn't imagine even Radd Stassen putting up with murder. Also, according to Mr. Stassen, Max had been annoying *Sarah*. Sarah being in the mood she was in, she probably hadn't been much annoyed, but that didn't change the fact that Jane watching Max hit on Sarah had no reason to push Verna into the path of a Lexington Avenue local.

Also, Verna had not been pushed. That much Phoebe had told anyone willing to listen.

I returned my suspicions to Max. Max-kills-Verna-for-threatening-his-secret-income had a sensible ring to it.

There was a dish of Halloween candy on a desk in the hallway on the way out of Dana's office. I took a handful and headed for reception. Tired had become exhausted had become catatonic. I had not been joking when I asked Dana if she wanted me to pass out while preparing posters. I was ready to pass out eating pumpkins.

From the general direction of reception a thin, shrill, exasperated voice said, "You *can't* throw up on the *carpet*. There's a *ladies'* room down the *hall*."

There was no answering voice. I gulped the rest of the pumpkins I'd picked up—grown people always look ridiculous eating Halloween candy—and wandered, hands in pockets, toward the sound of the shrill voice. I was surprised how quiet the office was otherwise. Dana and Radd Stassen at one end of the hall, the shrieker in reception at the other—nobody else was on the twenty-sixth floor.

"Oh my God," the shrill voice was saying. "You can't do this."

I turned the corner and stopped in the archway. On the other side was a grimacing, panicked Marilou Saunders, holding the doubled, wretching body of Sarah English in her arms.

It was' like looking at a Judy Chicago sculpture—Marilou in black silk, rhinestone buttons, and Max Factor Hot Promise red; Sarah in brown Woolworth slacks and long red double-knit sweater vest; Marilou's face distorted under terrified eyes; Sarah bent over at the waist and heaving.

"Dear Jesus," Marilou said. "I just walked in here."

I walked slowly to the blue plastic Dripmaster, poured myself a cup of coffee, and downed it. It seemed very, very important to be calm, and deliberate, and decisive. It seemed necessary to be awake, too, but there was nothing I could do about that. There were spangles like Christmas lights in front of my eyes. My head was buzzing. I had gone beyond the need for sleep and entered a world of waking dreams.

Otherwise known as sleep deprivation, hallucinatory state.

If I didn't get some sleep soon, I was going to start hearing things.

I threw the coffee cup into the wastebasket beside the Dripmaster. It bounced off the green metal rim and into the corner, staining the carpet. I retrieved it and placed it carefully in the trash.

Sarah was still doubled over at the waist, still writhing, still straining against Marilou's hands. Her pain got through to me, moving across my stomach lining in what I thought were sympathy spasms. Emergency lights were going off in my head, but I didn't seem capable of doing anything about them. I was swimming through molasses.

"The thing to do here," I said, "is call 911."

"You call 911," Marilou said. "I can't just *drop* her."

"Put her on the couch," I said. "Lay her down."

Sarah gave another heave, then a shudder, than a moan. Vomit was coming out of her in a thin brown stream, much too little of it for the violence of the convulsions that ripped through her every few seconds. Marilou, frail and shaky and probably on something, could barely hold her up, never mind move her. She braced her feet against the carpet and dragged.

I went to the desk, punched buttons until I figured out how to get an outside line, and dialed. I felt almost as nauseated as Sarah looked. The sight of her terrified me. I reached for my cigarettes and tried to think of a way to explain what was happening while still making sense. It couldn't be done.

I told 911 I had a matter of life and death—poisoning—and needed an ambulance. I told them I didn't know what caused the poisoning. I told them time was of the essence. I hinted at foul play. I told truth and lies with equal conviction. Nine-one-one had no reaction. Nine-one-one is a computer.

I hung up and sat down on the receptionist's desk. I found matches and lit my cigarette.

"Food poisoning," I told Marilou, trying to sound confident. "Salmonella. She must have had lunch someplace interesting."

"That's what I thought." Marilou had managed to get Sarah close enough to the couch to drop her. She brushed off her hands and shook out her dress. "It was the oddest thing. I come through the door and there she is, leaning over her shoes—"

"Standing up?"

"Yeah. On her feet and leaning over her shoes. You'd figure she'd have sat down. Or headed for the ladies' room, for God's sake."

"Maybe it came over her suddenly." I sounded like my grandmother.

"It must have." Marilou threw herself into a chair and started pawing through her purse. "Quaaludes," she said. "The only thing for a time like this is Quaaludes."

I shook my head. The little white Christmas lights had become strobe flashes. Incipient nausea was becoming actual. Every muscle in my face ached. I considered Marilou's hot pink ultrasuede handbag.

"You got any speed?" I asked her.

"You take speed?"

"I was thinking of something like caffeine pills," I said. "I—"

On the couch, Sarah had stopped wretching. She was lying rigid, twitching under the ungraceful folds of her clothes. My exhaustion nausea was joined by an eerie, sick feeling. I knew what was happening to Sarah. In a moment the twitching would stop and the rigidity would melt and the moaning would become a rattle. It would take longer and cause more pain than something simple like a knife.

"Jesus Christ," I said.

"What's the matter?" Marilou said.

I turned my head and tried to look at her, to concentrate on the emphasized makeup around her wide blue eyes and the thin strand of silver chain around her neck. The chain was under her dress, so as not to clash with the rhinestone buttons. The silver bangle on her wrist was a study in the non-Euclidean geometry of welded metal. The Quaalude was between the thumb and forefinger of her right hand. She was not holding a glass of water. She must have been intending to chew the thing.

"What's the matter?" she said again.

I pointed to the couch. The rattle had started. It was very low in Sarah's throat. It sounded like wood scraping against wood.

"What *is* that?" Marilou said.

The room was fluid and uncertain. Walls bulged and sucked as if they were breathing. The carpet made waves.

I thought of Sarah in Grand Central Station, eyes shining, hands tugging nervously against the strap of her shoulder bag, arrived in Mecca at last.

"I haven't had any sleep," I said.

"I don't care if you haven't had any sleep," Marilou said. She was shrieking, but it was very far away and I didn't mind. "Tell me what's going on," she said.

She grabbed me by the front of my sweater and shook me. I saw her shaking me but was unable to feel it. I saw the room and the waves and Sarah on the couch.

Somewhere on Mars, Marilou Saunders was contorting into the Platonic ideal of rage and frustration and fear. Her face was red. Her eyes were wild. Her Goldie Hawn hair was spiraling into Bride of Frankenstein static electric chic.

"Listen to me," she screeched. "None of this is my fault and I'm not going to get caught up in it, I'm not, so you'd better—"

"I'd better what?" I sounded drunk.

"What's *wrong* with her, McKenna?"

I made a last, valiant effort to get control of myself. I managed to stand up and straighten my back.

I thought of Sarah at Bogie's, Sarah in my apartment, Sarah kissing the taxi driver on the nose.

Sarah who had finally, *finally* won.

I tried to tell myself I could be wrong. I was sick. I was tired. I could be overreacting. I knew I wasn't. I knew because I could feel the hard scrape on my stomach lining that told me the same thing that had Sarah was about to get me.

I turned to Marilou Saunders, tried to focus, failed.

"Oh, hell," I said. "She's *dead.*"

Then I passed out.

NINE

Sound and light: cement-block echoes in a wind tunnel; flashbulbs and strobe lights and metallic fluorescent glare.

Give me a clamp give me a clamp give me a tube give me a clamp.

Squeak in one of the wheels. No sense of direction. *Get it out of her hand.* Somebody dropped the knife on the tiles.

It'll be all right if we hurry.

Get it out of her hand.

I need a wash I need a wash give me a clamp I need a wash blew the tube.

She's going to cut herself.

Give me a tube give me a clean tube.

Free fall roll. Tear in the throat.

It's home it's home give me a clamp.

I can't get it out of her hand.

You can't pump a goddamned empty stomach.

Red on white. Landscape of the earth after the explosion of the sun.

It's gonna work. It's gonna work anyway. Give me a clamp.

Nearly cut her goddamned finger off.

We're home we're home you can't pump a goddamned empty stomach but we're home give me a screwing clamp.

Tony Marsh said, "My face. That's the problem, my face. They take one look at me and think I'm a goddamned choirboy, not the Joseph Wambaugh type choirboy, the kind sings ten o'clock at St. Bernie's and then—"

There were no cigarettes on my bedside table. I felt the slick white metal, probing. Water glass (plastic), water pitcher (plastic), tissue box. No cigarettes. I opened my eyes to look at the tissue box. Kleenex.

On the other side of the room, Tony Marsh was saying, "That was the problem. I'd be on the street in uniform and this face and they'd pick fights. I mean, it *infuriated* them. The contrast, you know. And then I got the promotion and went into plainclothes and—"

I tried to sit up. There was a tube through my nose and down my throat and an IV in my arm. I felt feverish and achy and oddly disembodied. Except for the tube. There was nothing disembodied about the tube. I tried to say "Tony" and nearly strangled.

I must have made some kind of noise. Tony stopped midsentence. There was shuffling on his side of the room.

"Even if she is awake," a female voice said, "you can't talk to her."

"Not with that thing in her throat," Tony Marsh said.

"If she's awake, I can remove the tube," the female voice said. "But you still can't talk to her."

I gave it my best effort. I said, "I'm awake." It came out "lcomrska."

There was more shuffling on that side of the room, then footsteps, then two hulking figures coming through the light. The nurse was a nun with trigeminal neuralgia and a corrected harelip, dressed in something white and stretchy and a short veil. Tony Marsh was Tony Marsh. He looked as much like a homicide detective as Elmer Fudd looks like a brain surgeon.

"Maybe we ought to call Miss Damereaux in," Tony Marsh said.

The nurse did something to the tubes trailing up the side of my head, hooked her fingers at the plastic junction under my nose, and *pulled*. I felt like I was being eviscerated.

"There," she said. "If you pass out on us again, I'm going to be very angry."

"I want a cigarette," I said.

"No smoking allowed in the rooms," the nurse said.

"To hell with that," I said.

Tony Marsh coughed. "Maybe we ought to get Miss Damereaux and Mr. Carras," he said. "They've been waiting three days."

"Three days?" I said.

They ignored me. I lay very still. Since the nurse didn't seem like an ally, I waited until she had marched out of the room, leaving me alone with Tony. Three days? Did she say three days? I remembered Tony Marsh didn't smoke. I didn't remember much of anything else.

I tried to sit up again. Reality was fluid. The hospital bed was less manageable than a waterbed.

"Tony," I said. "Three days. What have I been doing here for three days?"

He said, "Sleeping."

I nodded. I needed cigarettes, and coffee, and chocolate, and Nodoz, and maybe even something stronger. My head was full of cotton candy.

"I know I've been sleeping," I said. "I figured I'd been sleeping. What am I *doing* here?"

Tony looked surprised. "You don't remember? You called 911."

I thought about that. I remembered calling 911. I remembered Sarah English dying. I remembered Marilou Saunders going to pieces in Dana's reception room.

"Okay," I said. "That takes care of Sarah. What am *I* doing here?"

"Sarah?" Tony said.

"Sarah English who died," I said. "Who I called 911 about. Marilou Saunders was standing there holding Sarah English and then we called 911 and we put her on the couch and then she died—at least she looked dead enough—damn, Tony, I *know*—"

"Marilou Saunders from *television?*" Tony said.

"Tony," I said.

Tony was shaking his head. "You called 911 and reported a poisoning," he said. "We got it all on tape. You can hear yourself if you want."

"Of course I called 911 and reported a poisoning," I said.

"And they got there and found you poisoned," Tony Marsh said.

"Found *me* poisoned?"

"Arsenic," Tony said sagely. "Are you having amnesia? If you're having amnesia, we should maybe call Dr. Heilbrun. You'll like Dr. Heilbrun."

It is remarkable how little patience I have when I'm sick and hungry and denied cigarettes. I was literally grinding my teeth. Worse, I was getting confused. Being confused scared me to death.

"Tony," I said. "You're a homicide detective. If you're here, somebody must be dead. I'm not, so who is?"

"Nobody's dead. Miss Damereaux thought you'd like to see a friendly face. We arranged it."

I tried again, cotton-candy head, swollen tongue, blocked nasal passages. "I was in Dana Morton's reception room. There was Marilou Saunders and she was holding Sarah English, who is somebody visiting me from Connecticut. Sarah English was all doubled over and trying to throw up. She—"

"You threw up," Tony said. "It was all over the carpet. How could you eat ratatouille quiche for *lunch?*"

"I didn't eat *anything* for lunch."

"You threw up a lot before we got you down here," Tony said. "That's what caused all the trouble."

"Tony," I said. "Where is Sarah English?"

Tony did his blink act. "You'll like Dr. Heilbrun," he said. "He pumped your stomach; he made it seem like football."

Phoebe had been down in the lobby getting coffee. By the time she got back to my room, I had given up trying to explain anything to Tony Marsh. I was lying in bed, going over and over the last things I remembered before passing out. Sarah. Marilou. The coffee. I thought about the coffee, and the arsenic. I thought about Sarah sick all over Dana's rug. I thought about cigarettes.

Nothing about that time was clear. Nothing would come together. I kept seeing disembodied pictures, like pieces of a rebus. Silver bangles. An empty patch of carpet. My head ached.

Tony paced the floor at the foot of my bed. "The problem we've got now," he said, "is reconstructing your day. Just in case this wasn't random. We don't know where you had lunch. We don't know who you had it with—"

"I didn't have lunch," I repeated wearily.

"You had ratatouille quiche," Tony said positively.

I let it go. Sarah had had ratatouille quiche. Ratatouille quiche was exactly what Sarah would have ordered for a first lunch in New York. I thought of that rattle in Sarah's throat. I gave it one more try.

"Coffee," I said. "It must have been in the coffee."

"In Dana Morton's reception room?" Tony asked. "We checked the coffee. We took that Dripmaster apart. And put it together again, of course. And gave it back."

I tried to concentrate. "Halloween candy," I said. "There was Halloween candy on a desk and I ate some of that."

Tony nodded. "Exactly," he said. "Halloween candy. It was crammed. Problem is, girl who had it on her desk says she's been eating it all week. Everybody in that office has been eating it all week. No problems."

"If you found arsenic in the Halloween candy," I said, "why ask me about lunch?"

"Fill in the gaps," Tony said. "Besides—"

"You're saying someone put them there just for me."

"Maybe not," Tony said.

"How'd they know I'd eat the stuff? Nobody offered it to me. I just took it."

"Well, there," Tony said. "You see the difficulty."

I closed my eyes and turned it over in my head. I couldn't make much of a case for the Halloween candy. How would Sarah have got hold of the Halloween candy? And no matter what Tony was trying to hand me, I knew Sarah was dead. I had seen her die.

Jane Herman. Sarah was supposed to see someone named Jane Herman.

I shook my head. Possible, but I didn't think it likely. That office had been deserted. Sarah hadn't been there when I got there. When would she have seen Jane Herman?

On the other hand, if she *hadn't* seen Jane Herman and she *hadn't* left the reception room, there had to have been arsenic in *both* the coffee and the Halloween candy. Which didn't seem very likely either.

There was a rattling outside in the corridor. Phoebe came bustling in, staggering under a D'Agostino's bag. I had a sudden, stabbing nonmemory of something—*something*—out of place. God only knew what.

Phoebe put the grocery bag on the chair next to my bed and bustled over to me. Then she stood on tiptoe so she could look into my face.

"Oh," she said. "Thank *God.*"

"Cigarettes," I said. *"Now."*

"Nick had to go downtown for an hour. I had the nurse call him."

"Cigarettes," I said again.

Phoebe frowned. "You can't have cigarettes in a hospital room," she said. "They don't allow it."

"Is this a private room?" I asked her.

"Of course it is. Nick and I wouldn't put you in with a lot of strange people."

"Do I look like I'm in an oxygen tent?"

"Now, McKenna," Phoebe said.

"Cigarettes," I said. I held out my hand.

Phoebe sighed and started rummaging in the grocery bag. "I *knew* you'd be like this," she said. "I got the call on the intercom and I thought, I'm going to get up there and the fool is going to start bellowing for cigarettes but thank God if she does because that means she's all right and here you are with a perfect chance to quit absolutely insisting on giving in to your addiction—"

She put the cigarettes in my hand. The pack was new and unopened and wrapped in plastic. The matches were from Lüchow's.

This time I managed to sit up. There was no ashtray, so I

dropped the spent match in the plastic water glass. Then I took the drag to end all drags.

Phoebe's grocery bag was sliding off the chair. I reached for it. I didn't make it. I leaned. I tottered. Only emergency action on the part of Tony Marsh kept me from falling out of bed. Phoebe got very stiff.

"If you need something," she said, "all you have to do is ask."

"Jelly doughnuts," I said.

"How about Zabar's chocolate croissants?"

She pulled a little white bag out of the larger brown one and tossed it to me. Tony Marsh glowered at both of us.

"I don't think she's supposed to be eating that sort of thing first thing," he said.

We both ignored him. Phoebe ignored him because Phoebe believes food is always good for you. I ignored him because, although I expected chocolate croissants to make me sick, I didn't really care. I ate three, told my stomach not to notice, and lit another cigarette. Procedures were falling into place. Plans of action were coming clear. I was feeling very alert and able to think of everything but explanations.

"Tony won't listen to me," I told Phoebe, "but you've got to. I was in Dana's reception room and Sarah English was sick and she *died,* for God's sake. I called 911 for her. And now she's missing. So you see—"

Phoebe was shaking her head. "Sarah English isn't dead," she said. "She's in Connecticut. She called me day before yesterday and said she'd heard all about you in the papers. She wanted to know if there was anything she could do."

The first thing Nick said was "Put that down."

I would have obliged him, but I had nothing to put that down on. I had managed to keep the nurse from confiscating my cigarettes, but she had been careful not to provide me with an ashtray, so all the time I was smoking I had to hold the cigarette in the air. I was holding it in the air when Nick arrived, sometime after eight o'clock. He looked like he hadn't slept in a week.

I had slept all afternoon. The chocolate croissants had finally backed up on me. I'd been sick and then exhausted and then asleep. The nurse tried to wake me for dinner but didn't manage. She tried to wake me for my vitamin pill but didn't manage that either. By the time I woke up, it was after seven, everyone else on the floor was drifting toward sleep, and I was feeling antsy and anxious and ready to go.

Except for the chocolate croissants, the scene with Phoebe and Tony didn't seem entirely real, any more than did the half memory, the *something*. Phoebe had left the grocery bag. I rummaged through it until I came up with a cheese blintz and a package of tortilla crackers. Fortunately, I didn't feel like eating much of either.

I had been dreaming about white-tiled corridors and harsh lights. I lay in bed smoking and thinking about the dream, and about Sarah, and about coffee and Halloween candy. Then there was Marilou Saunders. The way everyone was behaving, Marilou hadn't been in the reception room when the emergency squad found me there. Where had she gone? And why?

My head ached. I considered buzzing the nurse for an aspirin and decided against it. I would only get another lecture about smoking. Then Nick said, "Put that down," and instead of putting it down I tapped the ash into the plastic water glass and tried to smile.

Nick looked worse than awful. He looked dead.

"Jesus Christ," he said. "Don't *do* this sort of thing."

"Don't do what sort of thing?"

"Get yourself poisoned." He dropped into the armless, plastic upholstered chair and stretched his legs. The room was dark except for a tiny reading light above my bed. His face was in shadow. In my still-drifting state of mind, he looked like the protected interviewee in a "60 Minutes" exposé.

"I think," he said, "that I'm no longer going to take no for an answer."

"To what?"

"To opening negotiations about marriage. I've *had* it, McKenna."

I puffed at my cigarette. This was not the time to start talking about marriage. For one thing, the subject was more complicated than it might appear on the surface. For another, I was weak enough to forget that and say yes. I studied my cigarette ash.

"Did Phoebe tell you anything?" I asked him. "I'm not crazy, you know. They were there."

"I got here as soon as I could," Nick said. "I was here for about forty-eight hours straight and then I had to go downtown. I couldn't help it."

"You look like you were here for forty-eight hours straight," I said. "Did Phoebe *tell* you anything? Tony is making me nuts with this 'it's all in my head'—"

Nick leaned forward, intent, worried. "Phoebe told me everything," he said. "You want me to tell you everything?"

"Go ahead."

"You were alone in Dana's reception room when the ambulance got there," he said. "We checked everything—the coffee, the Halloween candy, the hard candy on Dana's desk, some cookies one of the typists had in a drawer. Arsenic in the Halloween candy. Period. I called Marilou Saunders before I got here. According to her, she never went anywhere near Dana's office that afternoon, she never saw Sarah except for that dinner at Bogie's, you must be hallucinating."

I cocked an eyebrow at him. The tone of his voice was heartening. "You believe me," I said.

"I believe there were other people in that room when you passed out," he said. "I don't know if I believe Sarah English is dead. She could have been very sick. She could have left. That's all."

"Why would she leave?" I asked him. "If she was so sick, *how* could she leave?"

"I don't know," Nick said.

"Do you believe me about lunch?" I asked him. "I didn't have lunch. Do you believe that?"

"I certainly believe you didn't have a ratatouille quiche." He smiled.

"How fast does arsenic act?"

"If the dose is strong enough, in minutes."

"Then it was in the coffee. I poured myself a cup of coffee and I drank it out of the cup. I chugged it. Nobody else got anywhere near it. The arsenic had to be be in the Pyrex pitcher thing."

"It was in the Halloween candy. We *checked*, McKenna."

"Whoever vomited ratatouille quiche had to be someone other than me."

"The police won't give you that," Nick said. "I will."

"That doesn't make any sense," I said. "Tony said people were eating the candy all week. And nobody got poisoned."

"Except you. And Sarah English, if you're remembering right."

"Of course I'm remembering right. But the Halloween candy was in an office in the back. Sarah was waiting in the reception room. The place was empty. Why would she go in back?"

"McKenna—"

"I had coffee when I first got to the office," I said. "Then I had it again when I found Marilou and Sarah. Somebody poisoned it while I was talking to Dana."

"All right," Nick said.

I sighed. There was an edge of reserve in his voice. I was ready to sleep again. I wasn't up to unraveling the emotional complexities of a summa cum laude graduate of the Harvard Law School with a tendency to believe that what is not admissible in court does not exist. I fastened on the one chink in his logical progression.

"You think someone tried to poison me."

"I know someone tried to murder you. Nobody's arguing that." He put his face in his hands. "I want to bundle you up and sneak you out of the country to a mountain in Switzerland. Leave it at that."

"I can't leave it at that," I said.

He looked up at me. "I don't think there's some murder plot afoot. I don't think we have another . . . situation on our hands. I think you got hit by a crazy. But that doesn't change anything, McKenna. Your story or Tony's, it's all the same to me. I can't handle thinking of you hurt and I can't handle thinking of you dead and I can't handle not knowing where this relationship's going. I'll give you enough time to get better and get out of here, but after that you have to make up your mind."

"*Nick.*"

He stood up, stretched his arms and legs, shook out the cricks in his back.

"They've got a cot in a room down the hall," he said. "I can stay there. Get some sleep."

"I'm not hallucinating," I said.

He sighed. "You just might not be," he said. "That's what worries me."

He took the cigarette out of my hand, turned off the light, and left the room.

TEN

Hospitals are required by law to allow patients who do not wish to remain in care to leave. That, of course, is only the law. The practice is often quite different. At Brandon Hill Medical Center, the practice was to keep me in my room and allow in anyone who bothered to knock.

"Knocking" may be a bit too metaphorical. Flesh and blood visitors were not the problem. Mail was the problem. At eight o'clock on the morning after I regained consciousness, the nurse brought in a tray of scrambled eggs, dry toast, and tea, and a purple and white Bonwit Teller bag full of mail. She put the tray in my lap and the bag at my feet, sniffed "Very popular, you are" like a member of the cast of *Upstairs, Downstairs,* then threw a small stack of message slips at my knees. "Messages day and night," she said. "Jennie doesn't have enough to do." She turned on her heel and walked out.

I gathered up the messages, wondering why nurses are always in such a bad mood. Long hours and low pay came to mind, but seemed too rational to believe.

I was not interested in my mail. I know what is in my mail.

I looked at the messages. My friends and business associates had decided I was not going to die. Expressions of concern and hopes I would get well soon were sparse and short. Hysterical demands to know whether I would be off my ass in time to meet this, that, or the other obligation were voluminous. The escapee from Hunter College reminded me I had a signing at Bogie's on Sunday, preceded by a talk at the 92nd Street Y (Wednesday), and a taping for Marilou's "Wake Up and Shine! America!" (tomorrow). There was also a photo session for *People* scheduled on Friday. *People* was underlined three times. I was not going to be allowed to blow a *People* story just because I'd been irresponsible enough to get myself poisoned.

Dana had made an appointment for me at Faces, the newest, trendiest, and most expensive makeup consultants in town, for Wednesday morning. She had arranged a signing for me at CrimeWave, a mystery bookstore, on Saturday. CrimeWave is in Cleveland. She had "managed" to get me a talk spot at the Fifteenth Annual Convention of Private Investigators—eight forty-five Monday morning on stage at the Calhoun (Texas) Sheraton. She was "endeavoring" to place me at Bouchercon, the annual mystery writers' convention, which was being held this year in Minneapolis.

Things were looking up.

I threw the message slips on the floor and reached under my mattress for cigarettes. I lit up with one of Phoebe's Tavern on the Green matches and lay back to think.

Maybe it was worse because I *could* think. I wasn't fuzzy. I didn't feel especially weak. Things that had seemed like badly constructed dreams the day before were now ominous and unsettling. Sarah English was dead. I had seen her dead. She had somehow disappeared. Marilou Saunders had also disappeared—at least from Dana's reception room. I didn't believe Tony Marsh wouldn't continue to check it out. I did believe Marilou would lie and tell him she wasn't there.

Marilou Saunders was the key.

I buzzed for the nurse. I waited. Nurses know who is dying and who is not. If you are not, they tend to let you buzz in vain for minutes at a time. I was occupying a very expensive private room and as such was entitled to some degree of courtesy. I waited one and a half cigarettes.

"Is there some way I could make a phone call?" I asked her when she stuck her head in my door.

She pointed to the wall over the night table. There was a pink kitchen phone screwed into it.

"Nine for an outside line," she said, disappearing.

I picked up the receiver and dialed nine for an outside line. I reevaluated my state of mind. I was no longer fuzzy, but I was still confused.

When I finally got through to Dana, she was exasperated and trying not to show it. Dana got into the office at nine-thirty. She did not appreciate phones going off in her ear the minute she stepped through her door. Besides, morning was her busiest time. She plotted in the morning.

I didn't bother to apologize. People who commit me to signings in Cleveland do not deserve to have me apologize.

"I need Marilou's direct line," I told her. "I—"

"If there's anything you need re the taping, I'll do it," she said quickly. "I don't want you saying a lot of stuff I'm going to have to get you out of later."

"It's not about the taping," I said.

"Clients are suicidal," she said. "Some half-assed movie producer tells them he wants to take all their merchandising rights in exchange for fifty thousand flat and he has to have story rights on top of it for a ten-million-dollar movie, and the client just sits there and nods like a drunk ninny."

"I don't want to talk about the taping," I shouted. Footsteps hurried to my door, stopped, hesitated. The nurse was trying to decide if there was something wrong with me.

Dana, too, hesitated. "What could you possibly want to talk to Marilou about?" she asked me. "What could anyone in their right mind want to talk to that lobotomized pharmacopoeia about if it isn't business? You don't even like her."

I got another cigarette. I needed Marilou's direct line. Without it, I wouldn't get through. The switchboard would assume that if I didn't have the number, I was not to be taken seriously. I didn't want to tell Dana what I was thinking—this mess had started in her offices, after all—but if I didn't tell her, she wouldn't give me the number.

"It's about the other day," I said reluctantly. "I know everybody thinks I'm crazy, but I know what I saw—"

"If you mean Miss English," Dana said, "forget it. She called me."

Sarah had apparently been running up quite a phone bill from Connecticut.

"You've been talking to Phoebe," I said.

"I've been talking to the police," Dana said. "For days. I know what you think you saw, McKenna, but, well—"

"Have you talked to Marilou Saunders?"

"Well," Dana said. There was another little pause. There was a cough. There was the sound of shuffling papers. "I've got a call coming in on the other line," Dana said. "I can't talk·now."

"Give me Marilou's direct line," I said.

"No," Dana said. "Don't forget your appointment at.Faces."

The line went to dial tone.

I put the receiver back in the cradle. I picked it up again and dialed the general number for the Network. I got (in chronological order) a switchboard operator, a division receptionist, and a "Wake Up and Shine! America!" secretary. All of them told me how *much* Ms. Saunders appreciated my support. I hung up again.

The problem with telephones is that they leave you too vulnerable. People can hang up on you. People can stare at their desk calendars or the *Times* daily crossword and forget you're there. If I was going to get anything done, I was going to have to get out of the hospital and back on the street. Or back in office buildings, which in New York amounts to the same thing.

I swung my legs over the side of the bed and headed for my private bathroom. The first priority was a shower. The second priority was clothes. The third priority was getting out before Phoebe could show up and stop me.

I had not considered the problem of money. Money is necessary everywhere, but in New York it is lifeblood. Nobody hitchhikes on Columbus Avenue. Nobody picks up hitchhikers on Columbus Avenue except police interested in making arrests for soliciting.

I stood in the middle of the room thinking about money and the alternatives to money. There was money in my apartment. I always kept a hundred dollars taped under one of the kitchen cabinet shelves in case I got robbed on the street. Unfortunately, my apartment was on Central Park West in the Seventies and Brandon Hill Medical Center was off Lexington in the Thirties. Total walking distance: two and a half miles. On a normal day I can do two and a half miles and not feel it, but this was not a normal day. I didn't feel weak, but I was going to before I went half that distance, and the walking wasn't going to be the worst of it. I would have window-shoppers to contend with. And traffic. And the lights at Columbus Circle, which are arranged to make it impossible for pedestrians to get from the park to the real city on any day when the New York Marathon is not being run.

I sat down on the bed and considered my options. The most sensible was to get out of my clothes, climb into my hospital nightgown, and ask the nurse to bring my pocketbook. Then I could get back into my clothes and, armed with my bank card, my American Express card, my Visa card, and (if I remembered correctly) forty-five dollars in cash, go looking for a cab. It was a wonderful plan. Unfortunately, it would take too much time.

It was quarter after ten. Visiting hours started at quarter after eleven. If there was any delay finding a nurse, or any delay in the nurse finding my bag, or an argument, I was going to run into Phoebe coming in. If I ran into Phoebe coming in, I might as well give up.

I lit a cigarette. I told myself I was giving myself a chance to think, but I was really wasting time. I always waste time when I don't know what I'm doing.

I was halfway through when there was a knock on the door and the nurse—my first nurse, she of the neuralgia and the corrected harelip—came sidling through the door.

"If you're going to escape," she said, "you're going to need help."

ELEVEN

I had to stop at three Chase Manhattan branches before I found
one with an instant cash machine. I had been unusually optimistic about how much money I had in my wallet. Credit cards I
had. Membership cards I had (Museum of Natural History,
Whitney Museum of American Art, Smithsonian Institution).
Money I did not have.

I did, however, have something new to think about. There
were advantages to be gained from too much newspaper publicity. My nurse had been proof of that.

"I've read all about you in the papers," she'd said. "And I
know what's been going on around *here.*"

"What's been going on around here?"

She was contemptuous the way only soap opera heroines can
be contemptuous. "They think you're hallucinating," she said.

"Well, that's what they thought the last two times, didn't they?"

That wasn't quite accurate—the second time they thought I
was hallucinating, the first time they thought I was *guilty*—but I
didn't correct her. She was bustling me down the hall, talking out
of the corner of her mouth in a low-whisper imitation of Bogart
doing a dying Sam Spade.

"We'll say you insisted," she said. "When we get to the desk,
act like you're insisting. Say things like 'If you attempt to restrain
me, I'll sue this hospital for illegal imprisonment.' Things like
that."

"I've never said a sentence like that in my life."

"Well, say it now. Then sign the form—sign out, it doesn't
mean anything. I'll call Dr. Heilbrun and you walk out. Just like
that."

"I have to wait for Dr. Heilbrun?"

"No, no, no," she said. "You walk out without waiting for Dr. Heilbrun. I can't stop you."

I said "Oh" and decided to go along. I was worried about her self-satisfaction level (very, very high), but it seemed a workable plan. I couldn't find any reason *not* to go along with it. She thought she was making herself part of a great adventure.

"Wait'll I tell my sister Maisie about this," she said. "Old cow. Thinks you don't get any excitement outside the emergency ward."

I found a cab fighting its way north on Third and got into it. It was going to take forever to get uptown, but I didn't care. Phoebe had to be on her way *downtown,* to the hospital and (she thought) me. Since Phoebe hasn't taken public transportation since her sales first topped two hundred thousand, I figured she was stuck. All I had to do was get to my apartment, feed the cat, and start on my rounds.

We stopped for a light at East Seventy-ninth Street, and I started rummaging in my bag for something to read. I usually carry at least three magazines and a book when I have to take cabs, but I hadn't taken anything when I went to see about Verna, and I hadn't been back to the apartment since. All I could find were three advertising circulars and an oblong manila envelope, crammed to bursting, with Brandon Hill Medical Center stamped all over it. The cab swung into the park, chugging angrily behind a bus whose driver stopped every three feet to look at the scenery.

"Look," the driver said. "I'm going to have a smoke. You going to bitch if I have a smoke?"

"Not if you give me a light," I said. I had the oblong envelope in my lap and a terrible feeling I was going to open it to find forty-five dollars wrapped in a rubber band. I tore the flap open and dumped the contents on my knees.

The driver threw me a pack of matches with two copulating lesbians on the cover and said, "These MTA guys, they don't care. They don't have to make time. Their paychecks come in regular."

I said something like "I guess" and pored through the stuff on my lap. No money. Keys, paper clips, a mini-screwdriver, a bent lipstick case, three inkless Bic medium points, four subway tokens, an American Express pocket calendar (last year's), but no money. Not even change. I wondered if I'd been relieved of it in the hospital or in Dana's reception room. So much for the honor of the bureaucracy—public and private.

"He's going down to Seventy-second," the driver said. "You want to go to Eighty-first Street? You don't want to go to Eighty-first Street, it's going to take all day."

"Go to Eighty-first Street," I said. The little silver thing was at the bottom of the pile, among the paper clips and tokens. I picked it up. It had a long stem (two inches) and a shorter branch. One end came to a flat, side-pronged point. The other looked as if it had been broken in two places. The break on the side had stretched the silver into a peaked tuft, like the peaks on birthday cake icing. The break at the end was sharp. It had edges.

"This is Central Park West," the driver said. "This is no problem from here."

"Right," I said.

I was still holding the silver thing in my hand when we pulled up in front of the Braedenvoorst. I had put the rest of the debris back in the envelope, but the silver thing bothered me. When the cab came to a stop, I got some money out of my pocket, threw it on the driver's seat, and got out. It brought the tip to $1.17, but I had too much on my mind to wait until he made change.

"Just like I always say," the driver said. "Women tip better than men. Always did. Always will."

"Right," I said.

"Wrong," Phoebe said. "What are you *doing* here?"

It was like someone coming up behind you and yelling "Boo" in your ear while you were standing at an open window on a high floor. I nearly fell off the curb.

"For God's sake," I said. "You're going to get me killed."

"You're going to get yourself killed," Phoebe said. "You're supposed to be in the hospital."

"I couldn't get anything done in the hospital," I said. I held up the silver thing for her to see. "You know what this is?"

Phoebe is not easily deflected. "I want to know why you're not in the hospital," she said, "and I want you to tell me while we're in a cab taking you back."

I did the only thing I could do. I ignored her. I waved the silver thing at her again.

"It was in this envelope full of stuff from my pockets," I said. "What is it?"

Phoebe squinted at it. "Oh," she said. "You were holding that when they brought you into the hospital. You wouldn't let go of it for anything. They kept trying to get it away from you and you wouldn't unlock your fingers. Not even drugged."

"I was holding it when I came into the hospital?" I said.

"That's right. I think you had it with you all the way in. It took a general anesthetic and some kind of sleeping shot to get you to give it up."

"But what is it?" I asked.

Phoebe regarded it solemnly. "It's a little silver thing," she said.

I said "Fine" and headed for the Braedenvoorst's archway. The Braedenvoorst does not have a door fronting the street. It has an archway, which leads to a courtyard. If you get through the archway (the archwayman has a gun), you are allowed to blunder around the courtyard looking for the one of fifteen identical entryways leading to your apartment.

Phoebe trotted along behind me, frantic. "But Pay," she said. "You can't just get up and walk out of a hospital. Your doctor has to okay it. I talked to your doctor yesterday. He said it would be nearly a week."

"Tell that to Public Relations over at AST," I said. "Tell that to Dana. I'm supposed to be in Cleveland in less than a week."

"Cleveland?"

The archwayman gave Phoebe a smile and a nod and me a curt

little wave. Phoebe does not live in the Braedenvoorst, but the staff wishes she did.

I strode through the courtyard, keeping the pace Phoebe expected of me. I was already exhausted, but it wasn't the time to show it.

"I couldn't get anything done in the hospital," I repeated, ducking into my entryway and heading for the elevator. "I call Dana to ask for Marilou Saunders's private line, she hangs up on me. If I call Marilou, *she'll* hang up on me. You can't get anything done on the phone."

"I don't understand," Phoebe said. "What do you want to get done?"

The elevator, an ancient brass cage, bumped to a stop in front of us. I popped the latch and pulled the metal grille out of the way.

"Most of what I want," I said, "is to tell that preserved-in-chemicals nitwit that I know what she's doing and she's not going to get away with it. For starters." I pushed the button for the fifth floor. "After that, I'm going to deck her. After that—"

"But Pay," Phoebe said. "You can't do any of that."

"You want to bet?"

"I don't have to bet," Phoebe said. "I know. They already talked to Marilou Saunders, last night, yesterday afternoon, sometime. Right after you woke up. She talked to Nick and she talked to Tony Marsh and then she just—disappeared. People have been looking for her all day and no one can find her."

I considered this. "No one can find her? You mean she didn't show up for work?"

Phoebe looked uneasy. "Well, no," she said. "She was there this morning. And she taped, of course. It's just that—"

"They wouldn't let anyone on the set and by the time the taping was over she'd disappeared," I said. "Like that."

"Well," Phoebe said. "Well. I guess so."

"Which means she isn't seeing anybody because she doesn't want to see anybody," I said. "What about her apartment?"

"She isn't at her apartment," Phoebe said. "At least, she

wasn't a few hours ago. Nick and I both went. And somebody from Tony Marsh's people."

"Ah yes," I said. "Tony Marsh's people." The elevator stopped on five. I let us out. "Why don't you tell me how diligent Tony Marsh's people have been about trying to get hold of Marilou Saunders?"

Phoebe stepped into the fifth-floor hall, dainty, decorous, careful. "Marilou Saunders may be a twit," she said, "but she's an important woman. You can't just go hauling off questioning her about God knows what just because one person says so when everybody else says not."

"Who says not?"

"Dana didn't see anybody but you," Phoebe said stiffly.

"Then Dana arrived after the other two were gone," I said. "Do you think I'm hallucinating? Do you really and honestly?"

"They talked to her once and she denied it," Phoebe said. "And there's no evidence she was there. Nobody else saw her."

I began looking for my apartment keys. "Don't start," I said. "I've had enough of this. I watch a perfectly innocuous woman get poisoned at my feet. I'm out for three days. I wake up and people who've known me forever and should know better keep acting like I've turned into a lunatic. I don't need this, Weiss."

"Patience," Phoebe said. "Listen to me. It would be one thing if Sarah English was really dead. Or even missing. But she isn't. She's back in Holbrook and she's fine. I don't know what you saw."

"Did you talk to her yourself?"

"Well, no," Phoebe said. "She left a message with my service."

"Anybody could have left a message with your service."

"Patience—"

"I know what I saw. I saw Sarah English die. I know that sort of thing when I see it. Especially these days."

"She went back to Holbrook and she's fine," Phoebe said. "You got poisoned by one of those nuts who doctor Halloween candy. She didn't want to be in the way."

I threw the keys on the floor. I'd tried every one of them. None of them fit my apartment door. Since this happens at least once a week, I picked them up again.

"Have you been in my apartment?" I said.

Phoebe nodded. "I just came from there." She held up her velvet string bag. "I was getting you some stuff."

"What about Sarah's stuff?"

"There wasn't any Sarah's stuff," she said. "She took it with her when she left."

"How?"

"What do you mean, 'how'?"

"How did she get her stuff if she didn't have a key?"

Phoebe stared at me. She stared at the keys in my hand. She stared at the rose and gray wallpaper in the hall.

"You didn't let her in," I said.

"No," she said.

"Nick didn't let her in or he would have said something. And the building people might have let her through the arch, but they wouldn't open my apartment for her."

"Maybe you forgot," Phoebe said. "Maybe you gave her the keys after all."

"I have three sets of keys. One I carry. One you carry. One Nick carries."

She took my keys out of my hand and fingered through them, frowning. Then she stood up very straight. "It's not here," she said.

"What?"

"It's not here. It's the one with the little knob at the bottom and it's not here. Maybe you did give it to her."

"I couldn't have given it to her. I came back here after we all had dinner and opened the door myself."

"Maybe you gave them to her later."

"Maybe someone took them out of my purse while I was lying on the floor in Dana's reception room."

Phoebe weighed the keys in her hand. She bit her lip. She shuffled her feet.

"We'll go to Holbrook," I said. "She's supposed to be in Holbrook—we'll go to Holbrook and find her."

TWELVE

Phoebe is better at these things than I am. She doesn't have to make lists. She had to borrow my bag, but that was detail. My bag was the only leather receptacle in New York capable of holding ten cans of decaffeinated Diet Coke, ten cans of Orange Crush, eight cream-cheese-and-olive sandwiches, two three-foot-long pepperonis, one quart of macaroni salad, six individual-serving bags of potato chips, a family pack of Chunky pecan bars, a pound box of Goobers, and three pieces of Phoebe's mother's kosher chocolate cake. When Phoebe traveled, she traveled *prepared*.

Nothing could have prepared us for our first sight of Holbrook, Connecticut. Phoebe had lived in cities all her life. I grew up in what people like my mother call "the country," by which they mean an exurban ghetto for the respectably ancient WASP rich. Holbrook was a provincial trading center for failing tobacco farmers, factory hands from Sikorsky Aircraft, small-time law firms, and the kind of Specialty Dress Shop that sells orlon imitations of fifties after-five dresses to women who want to look *different* at the Volunteer Fire Department's St. Valentine's Day Ball. We got off the train onto a creaking wooden platform, walked three yards to a disintegrating wooden station, and descended to what passed for a street. The street had been paved the way carpet is laid down in an irregular room. There were strips of dirt at the edges of the tarmac.

There were no cars in the parking lot, and no signs of town. Phoebe peered into the dusky gray afternoon, frowning.

"Taxi," she said. "Do you suppose there *is* a taxi?"

I pointed at a sign to a basement entrance to the station. It said, "Taxi Service in Holbrook and Suburbs."

Phoebe headed for the stairs under the sign, holding her skirts away from the filthy railing and above the grease-skidded stairs. She pushed open the door at the bottom of the stairs and marched in like a general.

"Taxi?" she asked the man sitting at the desk in the corner. The desk had one missing leg. It listed, threatening to spill papers and Michelob cans everywhere. The man in the chair had a White Stag ski jacket over his head. He didn't move.

Phoebe marched up to him. "Taxi," she commanded. When he still didn't move, she pulled the ski jacket away.

He was awake. His eyes were open. His breath was fouler than skunk cabbage. He gave Phoebe a wide grin and said, "Do I look like a taxi? Taxi's out back. Ford Impala, '67."

"You're the driver," she said.

"That's true," he said. "I'm the driver."

I got the cigarettes out of my pocket. I figured we were in for a lengthy impasse. Phoebe knew what she wanted, but she wasn't sure she wanted it from him. He was drunk. He intended to get drunker. He had a pile of unopened Michelob cans under his chair.

Phoebe took a piece of paper out of her pocket and consulted it. "Three twenty-three Halston," she said. "That's where we want to go."

"Three twenty-three Halston," he said. "Nobody's home."

"I'll leave a note," Phoebe said.

"Three twenty-one Halston, there you have somebody home. Cassie's got so many kids, she hasn't left the house 'cept for deliveries the past five years."

"Three twenty-three Halston," Phoebe said.

"New York City," the driver said. "Went away to become a big famous writer. Everybody's heard about it. Practically took out an ad in the paper, Sarah did."

Phoebe sighed. The man was not only drunk, but immobile. She obviously had no idea what to do with him. I did, but I wasn't sure I should. Did I *want* four six-packs of beer driving me through what could turn out to be traffic?

"How far away is it?" I asked him. "Could we walk?"

He cocked an eyebrow at me. Actually, he cocked half an eyebrow at me, because he had only half an eyebrow above each eye. Otherwise, he had burn scars.

"Anybody could walk," he said. "It's out the other side of town on the river. Mystery walk, we call it."

"Mystery walk?" Phoebe found this melodramatic in the extreme.

"Yeah," he said. "It's a mystery where all them babies come from. Ain't no men the women will admit to and ain't no women the men will admit to, see what I mean."

"Oh," Phoebe said. "Sort of like a housing project for unwed mothers."

"Unwed mothers?" I said.

"I think we ought to risk it," Phoebe said. "This is getting worse by the minute."

I started pulling out money.

Nothing about Sarah English was as I'd expected it to be. Instead of an apartment, she had one side of a vertically divided two-family house that was three years past "needing paint." I got out of the cab and stood in the unpaved road looking at it. There was nothing neat about it, nothing loving or well cared for or hopeful. Shutters that had once been green hung from single hinges at the upstairs windows. The mailbox swung rusted and dented from a single loose nail pounded into a splintering wooden post. The door, once red, looked fire-blistered.

I looked at Phoebe and said, "Nobody who ever lived in this house ever wrote a book."

"I know what you mean," Phoebe said. She peered into the mailbox. It was empty. "She took her mail. She has to have been home."

"If she ever gets any mail."

"Sears ads," Phoebe said. "And stuff from the Franklin Mint."

I let that pass. Somebody who lived in this house *had* written a book. For some reason I was never going to be able to pin down, Sarah had been the exception. She had smelled of failure and not failed.

I walked back and forth in front of the mailbox, kicking the rubber soles of my Adidases in the crack in the first cement sidewalk step. Sarah's situation had been worse than I'd imagined, needier. Looking at that house was an object lesson in the mechanics of entrenched despair. But Sarah had written a book and got it accepted for publication and come to New York. She had not been entrenched in anything.

I muttered something about "candidates for the gene pool" and started climbing the stairs to the walk, Phoebe trailing behind me. Somebody *was* home in 321, the other half of the two-family. Maybe Cassie, whoever she was, knew something about Sarah.

Phoebe chugged up beside me. "It wasn't so different in Union City," she said. "Not even different enough to notice."

"I've been to your mother's house," I said. "She's got clean curtains on the windows. She's got fresh paint if she has to paint herself. It's not the same."

"Not for her," Phoebe said. "You ever look around the rest of our neighborhood?"

"The rest of your neighborhood isn't the point."

"Keep things in perspective," Phoebe said. "She was an unusual person, making something out of herself starting in a place like this. Granted. Still, it can be done. I did it. Nick did it. It's not the equivalent of walking on water."

"I didn't say it was." I did, however, think it was. One of the drawbacks of growing up in "comfortable" circumstances is the tendency to be mystified at how anyone lives outside them. Another is the tendency to be overly impressed by people who not only do but make an escape besides.

I rang the bell at 323, listened to the silence on the other side of the door, then crossed the porch.

"Nobody home," I said.

"He told us that," Phoebe said. "She could be at work."

I said "Maybe," but without the sarcasm I would have used back in New York. Phoebe no longer sounded so sure of finding Sarah. She kept looking over her shoulder, off the porch and across the road to the river. That river looked lethal. It gleamed rainbow slick in the weak sunlight. It moved like something congealed.

On the other side of the door to 321, a child was crying. A woman's voice called out, asking Johnny to be quiet. Johnny didn't oblige.

The door opened on a chain, showing me a single unpainted eye and an unlikely tuft of pale brown hair.

"I haven't got it today," the woman said. "Come back Friday."

I was wearing olive drab fatigues and a "None of the Above" T-shirt I'd had made for the Carter-Reagan race and resurrected for Reagan-Mondale. Either bill collectors in Holbrook were an unusual lot, or the woman was blind.

"I'm looking for Sarah English," I said.

The pale brown hair quivered. "Not home," she said. "Out of town."

Phoebe pushed to the front. "We got a call from her," she said. "She said she was *back.*"

"Sarah called *you?*"

"That's right," Phoebe said.

Silence on the other side of the door. Labored breathing. The woman was a worse chain smoker than I. She took a long time thinking things through. She squinted the single eye at Phoebe and said, "You're from New York."

"That's right," Phoebe said.

"One of you someone named Caroline Dooley?"

I could see the will to lie rising like a balloon in Phoebe's head. She beat it back. "No," she said. "I'm Phoebe Damereaux and this is—"

"Phoebe *Damereaux?*"

The door slammed shut. The chain rattled in the groove. The door swung wide, revealing a short, gone-to-seed woman in a blue plaid flannel housecoat and half-teased hair, biting the butt of a cigarette. She advanced to the porch, staring at Phoebe's face, her mouth and nose and eyes twisted into an attempt to look too tough to be fooled.

"You're not wearing one of those *things,*" the woman said.

"Oh," Phoebe said. "Well. They're not very good for running around in."

The woman squinted and twisted again, letting us know she was thinking it over. Then she gave us a curt nod and an incongruously sickly sweet smile.

"Yeah," she said. "I'd have known you anywhere. I saw your picture in *People* magazine."

After a comment like that, Phoebe usually says something about how she hopes the person has also read the new Phoebe Damereaux. This time she didn't.

The woman was holding the door open for us, making ushering motions with her hands and the hanging flesh of her upper arms.

"Right this way," she said. "I had no idea Sarah knew so many famous people in New York. I mean, I guess she'll meet all the famous people now, won't she? Becoming a famous writer herself. Probably moving out of here and going to live in the city first thing, like she always wanted to. Not that I blame her for moving out of here."

We followed the hand and arm movements into a small living room. There was a tin wastebasket in one corner, a foot high and six inches across, filled to overflowing with cigarette butts and Ring Ding wrappers and used Pampers crumpled into brown streaked balls. There was a television set on an orange crate with a stack of yellowing newspapers beside it. There was a pile of empty Burger King wrappers on the couch. A listless baby sat in the middle of them, crying.

"I'm Cassie Arbeth," the woman said, hurrying over to the couch to pick up the baby. She held him sideways, like a sack of raw potatoes she was having trouble carrying home from the store. "I've been taking care of things while Sarah's in New York. Only the thing is, I can't watch everything every minute of the day, you know, and with my five and Sarah's Adrienne—"

"Adrienne?" The bottom of my stomach departed for Middle Earth.

Cassie nodded vigorously. "Adrienne's no more trouble than any of the others, she's only seven but she stays out of trouble, that one, but with Adrienne and my five to look after I don't have no time to be hanging around the porch, and with the noise they make and all—"

"Adrienne is Sarah's daughter," I said.

Something about the way I said it must have sounded odd. Cassie smirked. "Yeah," she said. "Adrienne. Told Sarah it was something else in a name, least 'round here, but Sarah was always reading *books.*" She sounded amazed that anyone would read books. "Sarah is a lot older than me," she said. She meant it as an explanation.

I looked at her more closely. Sarah had been in her late thirties. Cassie Arbeth looked fifty-eight.

"I'm twenty-four," Cassie Arbeth said. She rushed to the built-in bookcases under the stairway and extracted the only books there, four Holbrook High School yearbooks, each bound in imitation red leather with a raised plastic shield on the front. I looked at the dates and subtracted. She was only twenty-four. At most, twenty-five.

"Sarah isn't in any of these," she said. "Sarah was class of '65. God, that seems ancient to me. Not that Sarah showed her age so much."

Next to Cassie Arbeth, Hermione Gingold didn't show her age much.

"Wait a minute," Cassie said. She ran out to the porch and yelled "Adrienne!" at the top of her lungs. The word echoed down the empty street, finally drowning in the river. "The thing is," she said, coming back, "did you come from this Caroline Dooley or did you come about Adrienne?"

Phoebe was about to say something. I glared her into keeping silent. Cassie didn't remember what we'd said on the porch about looking for Sarah. I was beginning to think it was just as well.

"What did Caroline Dooley call about?" I asked.

"Well, it's like I was saying. I got a lot to do and I can't be watching everything every minute. I must've been out back sometime or else it was when I was asleep, you can get robbed on this street night or day, you know, but it could have been night, I told this Caroline Dooley that—"

"You had a robbery?"

"Sarah had a robbery. That's what I've been telling you. Sarah had a robbery and a bunch of stuff probably got taken, but I can't tell what. I called this number she gave me, but nobody's ever home—"

"Probably my number," I said. "I really haven't been home."

"Yeah, well," Cassie said. "I don't know what this Caroline Dooley wanted, but I told her I wasn't going to find it for her. Things are so messed up in there I'm never going to find anything. Not that things aren't messed up in here, you know what I mean, but it's different."

"Right," I said.

A small girl, pale blond and plain, appeared in the front doorway. Her hair was brushed sleekly back and caught with an elastic at the nape of her neck. Her dress was starched and pressed and clean. She looked like a Christmas angel come to roost at the town dump. She was very, very tense.

"Adrienne," Cassie said. "These are friends of your mother's."

Adrienne and I regarded each other. Usually, children take to Phoebe and avoid me. My height frightens them. My diffidence puts them off. With Adrienne English it was different. We each knew what the other was thinking. Better, we each knew what the other was thinking *about Cassie.*

I put out my hand. "I'm Pay McKenna," I said.

"How do you do," Adrienne said. She turned to Phoebe and waited politely.

"Phoebe Damereaux," Phoebe said. She sounded breathless. The sound of Adrienne's voice had been unexpected. Phoebe was concentrating on *me.*

Adrienne, too, was concentrating on me. "Is my mother going to be back soon?"

I thought of Sarah on Dana's reception-room floor, Adrienne in Cassie Arbeth's house. Somewhere there would be a juvenile authority and a list of foster homes, people who took children in for the money. Somewhere there would be a string of third-rate schools and a lot of subtle pressure to skip the college courses for something more "practical."

I thought of Sarah arriving in New York, eyes shining, the vicious circle broken. Finally.

"Actually," I said, "we're going to take you into New York with us."

Cassie said, "Oh, good."

Phoebe almost started smoking.

"Your mother is staying in my apartment. You can have a room of your own if you want."

"In New York City?"

"Right."

Adrienne regarded me. She was not so much solemn as cautious. Her eyes were very wide and very brown and very intelligent—intelligent enough to know from my manner that something was wrong, and that I had a reason, for now, for not telling her what it was. She made her decision on available facts, available prejudices: me and New York (unknown, but with possibilities), Cassie and Holbrook (known, but unbearable).

"All right," she said.

"Oh, good," Cassie said again.

"Dear Jesus," Phoebe said.

"Do you know how to make braids?" Adrienne said.

I got a hairbrush from my bag and undid the elastic at the nape of Adrienne's neck. I ignored Phoebe. Phoebe knew as well as I that Sarah had not come back to Holbrook without rescuing Adrienne from Cassie Arbeth—which meant she hadn't come back to Holbrook at all. If she hadn't come back to Holbrook, someone else had probably made the call saying she had. Which meant I was right all along. Sarah was dead.

"In front of your ears or behind?" I asked Adrienne.

"Behind, thank you," Adrienne said. "It's so much *neater.*"

I waved my hand in Phoebe's direction. "Go call the cab man back. I'll be done in a minute."

"We'll have to get some of Adrienne's things," Phoebe said. She looked murderous.

"We'll go next door and get them," I said.

Cassie Arbeth was on her feet. "I'll call the cab," she said. "I got something I want you to take to Sarah anyway."

She came back with a photocopy of Sarah's manuscript. She had spilled ketchup on the title page.

THIRTEEN

The inside of 323 was the first thing in Holbrook that reminded me of Sarah as I had known her. Toppled furniture and emptied drawers could not hide the essential neatness of that room, the shine of newly polished windows and freshly waxed floors, the precision of carefully hand-framed prints on the walls, the books (alphabetical by author) in orderly rows in a floor-to-ceiling plywood bookcase she must have had built or built herself. What she had not spent on the outside of the house she had spent on the inside. Walking through the door, you thought you'd entered an alternative universe.

Whoever had tossed that room had been bored before he started. The damage was minimal. The search, if there had been one, had been superficial. The desk was overturned and denuded of its drawers. The highboy, with its rows of birthday angels and ornamental plates commemorating childhood Christmases, was untouched. There had been no vandalism. Sarah's slipcovers, hand-sewn with a mediocre touch from cheap cotton calico, were new and clean and unripped.

Adrienne's room, one of the three small bedrooms on the second floor, was pristine. We left her there to pack dolls and pajamas and "good" dresses for the trip into the city, looked once into Sarah's bedroom (drawers pulled out in the imitation captain's chest, red cardboard jewelry box apparently untouched) and once into the third bedroom (sewing machines, sewing materials). Then we went downstairs.

"Television set," I told Phoebe. "That's all they could have taken. It's the only thing that should be here that isn't here. I don't think I've ever been angry at a thief before."

"You've lost your mind," Phoebe said.

"She had that jewelry box," I said. "It was probably all junk jewelry, but it must have meant something to her. And the creep didn't even open it."

Phoebe planted herself in a massive overstuffed armchair. "You're crazy," she said. "You can't do this."

I righted the desk and started replacing the drawers. Part of me said we should do what Cassie had not and call the police, but I couldn't see how it would help. It seemed much more important to return that living room to the antithesis of Miss Arbeth's. I couldn't think about Cassie Arbeth without getting ill.

"That woman is nine years younger than we are," I told Phoebe. "How could she let that happen to herself?"

"It's illegal," Phoebe said. "We're going to get arrested."

"What for?" I started picking up check stubs. I could hear Phoebe's foot tapping the floor behind me. Phoebe's feet almost never reach the floor when she's sitting in chairs. Tapping her foot takes an effort. Tapping her foot is a warning. "Doing this is better than leaving her in that," I said stubbornly.

"Sarah left her in that," Phoebe said.

"For three days. Because it was all she could do."

"If she'd wanted to bring her to New York, she could have brought her to New York. You certainly have enough room."

"If I'd known there was an Adrienne, I'd have invited Adrienne. She didn't even mention it. Not even in passing."

"You ever wonder why not?"

"This is New England, Phoebe. She didn't mention it because she didn't mention it. Maybe she was embarrassed about being an unwed mother. If she was an unwed mother. I don't know."

"What's going to happen if she turns up here looking for her daughter and that idiot next door announces the kid's been— For God's sake, Pay, this is *kidnapping.*"

I started on the ragged, pick-up-sticks pile of pens and pencils, making neat horizontal rows of them in the center desk drawer. I could hear Adrienne marching around above my head, pulling out drawers, moving things on wooden surfaces. "Even that hole I used to live in on Eighty-second Street was better built than this."

"Patience."

I turned to look at her. Her voice was stern, demanding, but she looked confused and hesitant. The last time I saw Phoebe (Weiss) Damereaux look confused and hesitant, she'd been matriculating at Greyson College for Women.

"She's not going to come back," I said gently. "This whole thing only makes sense if the rest of you are wrong and I'm right. You know that."

"I know you're taking that child across state lines, which makes it federal."

"You got a call from someone saying she was Sarah calling from Holbrook. So did Dana. But it couldn't have been Sarah calling from Holbrook. If she'd been here, she'd have seen Adrienne and that woman. Besides, look at this place. She'd have picked up. She wouldn't have made a lot of long-distance calls she could have made local in the city."

"Maybe she didn't come to Holbrook," Phoebe said. "That doesn't mean she's dead."

"What does it mean?"

"She could have dropped out of sight."

"Whatever for?"

"Obviously," Phoebe said, "she's got a whole life we know nothing about. We pegged her for an old maid, she's got a child. We had her scenarioed in an apartment, she's got half a house. She could have had all sorts of reasons."

There were postcards scattered over half the carpet. I started stacking them. "You don't believe it," I said, "and I don't blame you."

Phoebe sighed. "No," she said. "I don't believe that. But for God's sake, Pay, what do you think I'm going to believe? That someone murdered Sarah English? What for? That someone took her body and—"

"She was a small woman," I said quickly. "Five feet, very thin. She wouldn't be hard to carry."

"Why bother?"

"To get her out of sight. So people wouldn't know she was dead."

"What for? I mean, dear Lord, I know you're angry at Tony Marsh, but he's not an amateur. If he had any plausible reason for someone to kill Sarah, if he could find some solid evidence she was dead—and he was looking—"

"I'm not saying the reason's obvious."

"If they were going to move Sarah, why not move you? You're telling me this person had two people poisoned with arsenic on his hands and only moved *one.*"

"There wasn't any percentage in moving me. I practically live with Nick. I'm in the middle of a book promotion. I'm with you all the time I'm not with somebody else. I can't go missing without its being noticed."

Phoebe set her mouth. "The arsenic was in the Halloween candy. There are nuts like that all over the world. You ran into one."

"Where's Sarah English?"

"I don't know."

"Why is Marilou Saunders lying?"

Phoebe hesitated. She didn't like Marilou Saunders any more than I did. She certainly thought her capable of lying.

"Maybe Marilou Saunders was there," she said. "I can't see any reason for her to want to kill Sarah English."

"Neither can I," I said. "That's not the point. We couldn't see any reason for someone killing Julie Simms, but somebody did. Even if Marilou didn't kill Sarah, even if she didn't see Sarah— which she did—she's saying she didn't see *me,* that she wasn't even there, and I know that's a lie. I might have seen Sarah very sick and only thought she was dying. Until we find a body, that's always a possibility. But Marilou was also in that room and it's her word against mine."

"Maybe we ought to talk to Marilou," Phoebe said. "Maybe somebody ought to."

"I've got to tape her show Friday," I said. "I'll take care of her when the time comes. We won't be able to find her unless she wants to be found or Tony Marsh gets a subpoena, and I don't think we're going to get either. Who we have to talk to is Caroline Dooley."

"Caroline Dooley?"

"Caroline Dooley called here looking for Sarah. We can't trust the slob queen next door to remember what she wanted. I'm not even sure Cassie listened to what Caroline wanted. The only thing we can do is ask Caroline herself."

"Oh," Phoebe said.

"Logical," I said.

"I don't see what good it's going to do," Phoebe said. "But—"

There was a sound on the stairs. We both turned to see Adrienne descend, dressed in fresh starched yellow cotton, with a soft gray cardigan over her shoulders and a child's cardboard suitcase in her hands. She walked down the stairs as if she were balancing the traditional book on her head.

She reached the bottom of the stairs and put her suitcase on the floor.

"I thought it was better to change," she said. "The other dress was wrinkled in the back."

"Good idea," I said.

Phoebe wagged her head, considering. "Do you like cheese blintzes?" she asked Adrienne.

Adrienne had never heard of cheese blintzes. She was, however, "very fond of cheese."

FOURTEEN

It is not responsible to leave a seven-year-old child alone in a large, unfurnished Manhattan apartment. Phoebe knew that. I knew that. Even Nick would know it when he finally showed up. Nick was going to be the biggest problem. Nick was going to swear. Nick was going to shout while he was swearing.

We sent Adrienne down the long hall in search of a room she liked. I explained about the lack of beds. Adrienne nodded solemnly, humoring me.

I watched her progress through the living room, hoping she'd pick something with a view—the room I'd given Sarah, for instance, that overlooked Central Park. She was very small in Myrra's formal living room. She was also very straight-backed.

"You're sick," Phoebe said as soon as the child was out of sight. "You've been running around all day. You can't go running around all night."

"I tried phoning," I said. "I couldn't get an answer."

"What makes you think going over there is going to be any better? If Caroline isn't home, she isn't home."

I pointed to Phoebe's watch. "It's six-thirty. She's probably on her way home from work. Everybody is on their way home from work."

"I'll go over there," Phoebe said.

"I can't cook," I said.

"Oh, God," Phoebe said. "You've got a six-pack of diet soda, two bottles of Heineken dark, some Devon cream, and a yogurt. We have to go to the store. Children need vegetables."

"Santini's delivers," I told her. I got a scarf out of the closet and draped it around my neck, concession to Phoebe's as yet unstated fear that I would Catch a Chill. "I'll probably get there right when she does. I'll ask my questions and come home."

"You could wait to call later in the evening."

"No."

"Patience—"

"Hold Nick off until I get back," I said. "Give him something that will make him lose his voice."

Adrienne appeared from the back hall. "You really don't have any furniture," she said, giving me a half-shocked and thoroughly admiring look. "Not *any.*"

Phoebe held her head. "I'll call Santini's," she said. "I'll make chicken. When you get back here, you'd better be ready to eat chicken."

I hit the courtyard at a run, the street at a sprint. I was in the cab with the door closed before I saw the "No Smoking" sign. I considered lighting up anyway and telling this idiot that with two inches of bulletproof plastic between us, he wasn't going to come in contact with anything he was allergic to anyway. I didn't. I was too tired to argue. Even with Phoebe's train provisions, I felt as if I hadn't had enough to eat. My stomach was raw. There was something in there like sand, scratching me up.

I had put on a good act for Phoebe, but I couldn't fool myself. I *was* exhausted. Worse, I was beginning to get a sneaking suspicion I should never have left the hospital. I wondered what near-fatal arsenic poisoning did to you. Was there something still going around in my bloodstream? Was my stomach going to feel like this forever? Was arsenic like LSD, with a potential for flashbacks? What would an arsenic poisoning flashback consist of?

I was trying to force myself to think of the Best Possible Question to ask Caroline Dooley when we stopped for a light at West Seventy-second. The bulletproof partition slid open. The driver was smoking something cheap wrapped in Connecticut tobacco. I got out my cigarettes.

"You don't look dead to me," he said.

"What?"

He passed me a copy of the *Post*. I stared at the back-page picture of a man doing something hostile to a football.

"Up front," the driver said, pulling into the park. "That's you, right?"

Considering some of the things the *Post* has said about me— and some of the pictures it's run—I thought the better part of valor would be to throw the damn thing at a rock formation, littering laws or no littering laws. I could not, however, help myself. I turned it over. I looked down at one of those anonymous stretcher pictures that run periodically on the front pages of all New York newspapers, and a boxed inset of the Doubleday studio portrait from the back of my book. I looked up at the headline. I winced.

"HOSPITAL COVER-UP" was in 36 point. "WHY THE LOVE GIRL'S DEATH MUST REMAIN SECRET" was in 18. "Story on page 8" was only in 10 point, but I didn't care. I had no intention of turning to page 8.

We pulled out onto upper Fifth Avenue, world of museums and art galleries with rents higher than their incomes. I considered engaging the cab driver in a discussion of Manhattan rents. Since the average "junior studio" (closet with hot plate) was running seven hundred a month at last count, discussions of rents in Manhattan can be cathartic.

The cab driver had his own idea of catharsis. "It looks like you," he said. "But you're not dead."

"How can it look like me? That picture is so small, you need a magnifying glass to tell if it's male or female."

"Page 8."

I turned to page 8. They had the complete set of "at-home" publicity stills I'd had taken for AST. I made a note to ensure that my escapee from Hunter College escaped permanently.

"So that's you," the driver said.

"Right," I said. "That's me."

"And you're not dead," the driver said.

"Not yet." But soon, I thought. Nick was going to kill me.

"Yeah," the driver said. "I always thought the *Post* was full of shit."

Everybody does.

We pulled up in front of Caroline's building, one of those cement block and glass cubes in the Forties, almost simultaneously with the fire trucks. A small knot of people had gathered on the sidewalk to watch. Other people were streaming out of the building or being held up by the doorman. I gave the cab driver five dollars and climbed into the street, craning my neck to see if there was smoke coming from one of the upstairs windows. There was nothing.

"Hope nobody was cooking you dinner," the driver said.

I edged closer to the building. The crowd was well-dressed and polite—Manhattan fires attract the kind of spectator who would feel it beneath himself to watch if he lived anywhere else—but it was welded into a solid mass. It was difficult to make my way through. The firemen were running a relay race—first into the building, then out again, then in again, always single file—but none was covered with soot or sweat or anxiety. The air of emergency was routine.

I wedged myself between a woman with Adidases and briefcase (low-level management, Adidases were last year) and a man whose briefcase was so slim it couldn't have held more than a credit-card slip. They were standing at the police barricade.

"Somebody was in there," the woman said. "He's burned to a crisp."

"Nobody is burned to a crisp," the man said. "The human body doesn't work that way."

The doorman stepped into the crowd and shouted, "Fourteenth floor, fourteenth floor."

I looked through the crowd. I looked at the building. I squinted, trying to see to the end of the block in the distorting light of arc lamps. I turned toward the river and saw Caroline Dooley, her arm linked through the arm of an insufferable middle-aged man in herringbone tweed.

I abandoned my attempt to get next to the police line. I headed out of the crowd, trying to look bulky as well as tall, to give myself the advantage of being intimidating. Unfortunately, I am only intimidating to small women and men with ego problems. By the time I got to the edge of the crowd, Caroline Dooley and her friend were already wedging themselves into the mass.

I caught Caroline by the elbow and pulled her back.

"I was just coming to see you," I said.

She stared at me, stupid. "My *building's* on fire," she said.

"I don't think it's that bad," I said.

"Why don't we go up and ask," the man said.

"Pay McKenna," I said. I held out my hand.

He took my hand, smiled, and said, "John Robert Train."

"Oh, *God,*" Caroline said.

"John Robert *Train?*" I said. "Verna's John Robert Train?"

"They've been divorced for *years,*" Caroline said.

"There she is," the doorman yelled. "Miss Dooley from 1426. I don't know who you think died up there, but it ain't her, because she's *here.*"

FIFTEEN

The fire chief was a weathered, cadaverous man with buckteeth and the light of passionate bigotry in his eyes. He had no more use for his crew (two women, two blacks, two Hispanics, and a white man with an Appalachian accent) than he had for Ms. Caroline Dooley, Woman Posing Around as Big Executive. He stood in the glass and marble foyer, staring at the rococo ceiling and shouting.

"Smoke inhalation," he said. "*Smoke* inhalation."

I had attached myself to Caroline like a Siamese twin. The fire chief didn't notice. Neither did the super, the doorman, or the two underage patrolmen who had been hauled in to provide a Police Presence. John Robert Train eyed me dubiously, but he wasn't about to say anything. He had troubles of his own.

The fire chief led us to the elevators. The super, the doorman, and the two policemen got into the east elevator. The fire chief, Caroline, John Robert Train, and I got into the west. We punched "14." It followed "12."

"Smoke inhalation," the fire chief said again. "She's pretty singed, but it wasn't that. They die by fire, you can tell. They get this look on their faces."

"Oh, God," Caroline said.

"This one looks peaceful," the fire chief said.

"Who?" Caroline said. "*Who* looks peaceful?"

"What we can't figure is why she didn't move," the fire chief said. "Found her just sitting in a chair. Whole thing about to fall into ash and sticks the minute you touch it, but there she is. Now why didn't she get out of the chair?"

"Smoke inhalation," Caroline said, sarcastic.

"Nah," the fire chief said. "With smoke inhalation, they're

overcome while running for the door. You find 'em passed out on the carpet."

The elevator stopped on fourteen, opened, deposited us in the hall. Blank beige walls bordered thin maroon carpet and surrounded maroon metal doors. It looked like the Locked Ward in a not particularly expensive institution for the treatment of senile dementia.

The east elevator disgorged the Nominal Officials. As if on cue, the fire chief turned his back on us and tramped around the corner in the direction of 1426.

"We didn't find any cigarettes," he said to the ceiling. "The oven wasn't on."

"In his last life he must have been an *art* director," Caroline said. "What is he *talking* about?"

John Robert Train coughed. It was a very discreet cough, meant to be heard only by Caroline, but it made the doorman and the two policemen jump.

"I think he's saying the fire started in your apartment," John Robert Train said.

"The fire started in my apartment and there's a woman in my apartment?" Caroline said. "For God's *sake.*"

We turned the corner and came to a stop in the middle of the hall. The door to Caroline's apartment was open, looking black and scorched and loose on its hinges. All the other doors were as maroon and pristine as the ones near the elevator. The fire had not only started in her apartment, it had been *contained* in her apartment.

We crept closer, reluctant to move too quickly, reluctant to arrive. Behind us, the elevators opened again. We heard the first of the ambulance men.

"That's a foldable stretcher," one of them said. *"Fold* it."

We advanced. "Dear Jesus," Caroline said. "What is this? What's going on in my life?"

She went to the doorway and stood peering into the smoke.

"Paper," she said. "More *paper.*"

"What?" I asked her.

"Paper," she said again. She gestured into the smoke. "Somebody took all my bills and *burned* them."

The bills had indeed burned. There was a charred, sodden pile of them in the middle of what had been a white carpet. There was what might have been more of them on a chair, burned into a hollow in the paisley damask.

"The *Starrunner* manuscript," she said. "Oh, *Christ.*"

The fire chief came out of the smoke, stamping his cleats into the carpet.

"You see what I mean?" he said.

"I don't see anything," Caroline said. "I see my apartment burned up. That's all I see."

"Just a minute," the fire chief said. He turned away and stomped back into the smoke.

Caroline turned to me, eyebrows arching. She wanted to leave. I didn't want to go. It had been a long time since I allowed manners to interfere with getting something I really wanted. I stared back.

"What are you doing here?" Caroline said.

"I came to see you."

"Well, yes," Caroline said. "I know that. But—"

The fire chief came back. This time I knew the stomp was commentary, not habit. He wanted to destroy that carpet. He wanted to destroy all the white carpets in Manhattan and all the pinko liberals who bought them.

"No cigarettes," the fire chief said. "No oven on. Fire started in the middle of the room someplace."

"In the middle of the room *some*place?" Caroline said.

"We did some pretty heavy hosing," the fire chief said. "Things got moved around."

The ambulance men came up behind us, stretcher finally folded. We let them by.

"We'll be able to tell when the lab gets through," the fire chief said, "if you see what I mean, but right now all we know is the fire started in the middle of the living room. Maybe this friend of yours—"

"Whoever it is, is not a friend of mine," Caroline said.

"She's here," the fire chief said. "She's the only one here. Who's got keys to your apartment?"

"I have keys to my apartment," Caroline said. "The super has keys to my apartment. That's it."

"You don't smoke cigarettes," the fire chief said.

"Filthy habit."

"With cigarettes, that's something we know about. People go to sleep. I smoked for thirty years, never fell asleep with a cigarette in my hand, never could, but these people—"

"Why don't you *identify* her?" Caroline said. "Why don't you find out who and what was in my apartment?"

The fire chief set his face.

I moved around them, cautious and fey. I knew this conversation. It could go on forever, and probably would. The fire chief couldn't say he thought the fire had been set. If he did and it hadn't been, or wasn't proved, Caroline could sue. Either Caroline had set the fire herself and was being smarter than she'd ever before shown any evidence of being, or she didn't know what was going on. I left them to their impasse. I thought they would enjoy it.

Caroline had a lot of high-tech furniture with metal frames and white cushions. The cushions were wet and gray-looking. The metal was burned black. I pushed aside a chair that had been toppled in the confusion of men and hoses and moved closer to the ambulance men. They were bending over a body in a chair near the chrome and glass coffee table, swearing.

"You folded the damn thing," one of them said. "Now unfold it."

"I'll unfold it if you'll deal with *that.*"

"I'm going to get the police to deal with *that,*" the first one said. "I'll give them the gloves and they can pick it up."

"Damn thing's broken," the other one said.

There was what looked like a paper paste sculpture at my feet, the kind they teach you to make in kindergarten because all the materials can be found around the house and are nontoxic. I leaned over to look at it. It was more paper, but what kind was impossible to determine. It had been shredded into confetti. And burned.

Caroline's voice sailed through the smoke. "Last Friday," she said. "Somebody came into my office last *Friday* and tore the place up with a razor blade, for God's sake, and now you're trying to tell me— Oh, dear. Last Friday. The keys—"

Last Friday was the day someone had filled me full of arsenic. I turned toward the sound of Caroline's voice. It seemed important, terribly important, to get to Caroline and find out what had happened in her office.

Behind me, the ambulance men grunted, heaved, and staggered backward. I moved out of the way. I had to move backward, away from Caroline and the door, because the ambulance men were carrying the stretcher at a tilt and in a hurry.

They should have been carrying a body bag. The woman on the stretcher was not so much burned as disintegrating. Her face was slack and shriveled. The skin under her fingernails was black.

For the first time, the smell of her penetrated the smell of smoke and chemical extinguisher, filling my nostrils with an odor so sickly sweet it was almost a taste.

That woman had been dead for days. The policemen, young as they were, would know as soon as she passed them. The ambulance men knew already, but weren't making waves. The coroner wouldn't have to think twice.

I looked down into Sarah English's blank, unyielding eyes and wondered if I should call Tony before I called Nick, or make it the other way around.

SIXTEEN

What Nick said was:

"It's the arrogance I can't believe. The blind, stupid, all-powerful arrogance."

I closed my eyes and put the back of my head against the disguised cement block of the wall. We were in the lobby of Caroline Dooley's apartment building. That was what the two young patrolmen thought of as "neutral territory." They couldn't leave us in Caroline's apartment—not only had the fire made it uninhabitable, the body had made it a possible crime scene. They didn't want to take us to the nearest precinct. I might be some kind of nut, no matter what Tony Marsh said. They might be liable for a charge of false arrest, assuming they could figure out who to arrest.

The cigarette between the fingers of my right hand felt like it weighed five pounds. My wrist felt close to cracking. It was all happening too fast. My emotions were having a hard time catching up. Sarah English in Dana's reception room. Sarah English in Caroline Dooley's apartment. Sarah English in Holbrook. Sarah English.

Once upon a time, I wanted to play the big, sophisticated New York writer. Once upon a time, I, as Nora Ephron said about Helen Gurley Brown, only wanted to *help*. Dear Jesus.

"We've got to *talk* about this," Nick said.

I opened my eyes and looked at the cigarette in my hand. The ash was an inch and a half long. I tapped it into a potted plant.

Caroline Dooley and John Robert Train were on the other side of the lobby. John Robert Train looked resigned but in control. Caroline looked furious and incredulous. Neither of them was speaking to me.

"What I want to know," Nick said, "is what you intend to *do* with her."

I sat up, bent forward until my head was between my knees, bounced. It didn't help to clear my head, but it made me think I was doing something.

"What I intend to do with her," I told Nick, "is keep her."

"You're out of your *mind,*" Nick said.

I came up for air. "I don't see why," I told him. "Sarah's dead. Adrienne's alone. What do you want me to do with her? Let the juvenile authorities have her? You're the one who told me those places were snake pits. Give her back to Cassie Arbeth? You haven't seen Cassie Arbeth. Loan her the money for a bus ticket? To where?"

"Stop making the argument ridiculous. You can't just take a child. You have to go through channels. The law makes you go through channels."

"Possession is nine tenths of the law." I was quoting.

"I don't think you can possess a person," Nick said. "And there may be relatives."

"We'll check relatives. I'll be good about relatives."

"You can't tell me you've fallen for this kid in less than a day."

"It's not her," I said. "It's Sarah. Something I owe to Sarah. Don't make me explain it now, for God's sake. It's too complicated."

"Phoebe says it's liberal guilt."

I ignored him. He turned to look out the great plate-glass windows at the street. A thin rain was beginning to fall. The ruts and mounds—results of eighteen months of attempting to construct an office building next door—were turning to mud.

"You're a public personality," Nick said. "You've got a reputation for getting involved in crime." I started to look indignant, but he frowned me down. "You get involved in the right end of crime, but that's not the point. The juvenile authorities are very conservative. They still think of the perfect family as a clone of 'Father Knows Best.' If you really want to play foster mother to this kid, assuming we can untangle the legal ramifications of your taking her across state lines in the first place, which I doubt—"

I got up and walked away from him. There was activity in the street: two blue-and-whites and an unmarked car I knew was a police car only because Tony Marsh got out of it. A beefy, hang-dog-looking man got out of it with him. I had never seen Tony's partner before.

I didn't really know I wanted to keep Adrienne with me. I just knew I had to get her out of Cassie Arbeth's house. And I did.

On the other hand, keeping her with me did not sound like a bad idea, now that I'd thought of it.

I pointed into the street. "They're here," I told Nick, although he was perfectly capable of seeing them himself. "God, I wish I knew what was going on. This whole thing is so crazy."

I rubbed the flat of my palm against my lips. The scene outside had turned into a dance. Our two patrolmen stood just outside the door, hands folded over their chests. Four more patrolmen paced in the street. Tony Marsh and his partner leaned against the unmarked car, staring into the sky. I wondered what they were saying to each other out there.

"I couldn't have left her there," I told Nick. "You should have seen that house. You should have met that *woman.*"

"Pay—"

"Maybe you had to be there," I said.

Outside, the dance came to an end. The patrolmen made a wedge and let Tony and his partner through, as if protecting them against the ghost of popular resistance. The door opened. The patrolmen flattened themselves against the inside wall. Tony and his partner came in, bride and groom in a parody of a military wedding.

Tony looked around the lobby, spotted me, and said, "Miss McKenna. Miss *McKenna.*"

It took half an hour to get it straight—times, people, places, conjectures. Tony's partner crossed the lobby to talk to Caroline and John Robert Train. Tony didn't seem to be interested.

"We got the body down to the ME's office and put a rush on it," he said. He looked proud of himself for saying a sentence like that. "They'll call us here and give us the results if they get them in time."

"Are you going to go up and photograph things?" I asked him. "Are you going to take fingerprints?"

"Probably." He shrugged. "With all the moving around and the fire hoses and things, I don't see what good it'll do, but we'll do it. Have to keep up the form."

"Of course," I said.

"It could still have been a nut," Tony Marsh said. "You ate Halloween candy. She ate Halloween candy."

I snorted. "Why move the body?"

"The body could have moved itself," Tony said placidly.

I got up and headed for the elevators. "I've heard all this before," I said. "It didn't make any sense before and it doesn't now."

Caroline glared at me from across the lobby. "It's all *her* fault," she said. "She's some kind of nut."

I stabbed at the elevator button. Tony and Nick caught up to me, Tony puffing, Nick's eyes doing the whirligig that announces imminent explosion. I didn't care. I'd been listening too long to this rigamarole about accidents and crazy people. I knew what kind of case Tony *wanted* it to be. I knew he didn't want to get tough with Marilou Saunders. I knew he was embarrassed at the possibility that he might have been wrong. None of that changed anything, any more than Nick's not wanting me to be involved in another murder case changed anything.

"You can't go up there," Tony Marsh said.

"Yes, I can." The elevator doors slid open. I held them for Tony and Nick, stepped in myself, and punched "14." The doors slid shut again. "There's something I want to show you two, and then I'm going to tell you both a story. If you don't want to listen, you can both go to hell."

"You're interfering in a crime scene," Tony said, a little hysterical.

"I thought maybe there wasn't any crime scene," I said.

The doors slid open again. We got out, threading our way through a knot of people waiting to go down. The will to privacy

ad been breached. All along the hall, doors were open, tenants
ere gathered in clusters, pets were free to scratch and mark and
⌐xcrete on the hall carpet. As we approached Caroline Dooley's
door, a thin blond woman in white silk lounging pajamas and
gold wedgies broke away from her group, held a pointing finger
in the air, and screeched,

"That's *her*. That's the dead girl."

I took the keys from Tony Marsh's hand, found the one for
Caroline's apartment, gave myself a few seconds to be impressed
with the car key (it costs more to keep a car in Manhattan than it
does to rent an apartment most other places), and let us in. The
blond woman had come to a halt about five feet from us. I didn't
want to give her a chance to get moving again.

I pushed the two men into the lingering smoke and shut the
door behind us. The air was much clearer than it had been. It
was damp and cold, but not suffocating. I looked at the cleat
marks on the carpet and the piles of blackened papers and the
streaks of gray and dirt on the once-white walls.

"Look at this place," I said. "Just look at it."

Tony Marsh shrugged. "It's a mess. I expected it to be a mess."

"Sarah English was dead before she got here," I said. "Dead
for days. The ambulance men have been saying that over and
over. Don't try to hand me anything."

"She could have died here," Tony Marsh said dubiously.
"Days ago—"

"And Caroline Dooley lived with a corpse in her apartment for
days? It makes more sense to say she died somewhere else and
someone brought her here and set fire to the place. To her."

"He can't say that until he knows," Nick interrupted, "and he
isn't going to know until the fire department gets finished
with—"

"Bullshit," I waved my hand at the room. "Look at the place.
Three piles of paper on the floor. Bills. A manuscript. Something
else. Those are burned. The couch is a little scorched. Everything
else is messed up from smoke and fire hoses and people's shoes.
Somebody set fire to three piles of paper and that was it. And if
the fire department doesn't agree with me, I'll go to New Jersey."

Tony was frowning, thoughtful, childlike, disturbed. "That doesn't make any sense," he said. "If what they wanted to do was conceal the body, three piles of paper isn't going to set a serious fire fast enough—"

"I don't think anyone was trying to start a serious fire," I said. "They'd have used lighter fluid, or kerosene, or something. I think somebody was trying to get the body *found.*"

"All they had to do was leave it here," Tony Marsh said. "Miss Dooley would come home and find it."

"Right," I said. "Okay. I don't have an answer to that. But consider this. Caroline was talking before about her office being vandalized last Friday afternoon. Which means she couldn't have been there, which means she could have been somewhere else, which means she could have been in Dana's office—"

"Whatever for?" Nick said. *"Whatever for?"*

I retreated. "I don't know whatever for," I said.

Tony looked around the room, staring at the blackened piles of papers. They *were* the only things seriously burned. Everything else just looked wrecked.

He stepped across the carpet and planted himself directly over the sodden pile of burned bills.

"Crumple up a lot of paper and drop a match in it," he said. "It's possible."

"It still comes down to whatever for," Nick said stubbornly. "You've got a murder. You've got a removal of the body. You've got a fire. You might—"

"We might have two murders," I said. "And we might have whatever happened to Caroline's office."

Nick glared at me. "You're getting *baroque,*" he said stiffly.

"What I think," Tony Marsh said. The intercom buzzer went off. Tony looked both Nick and me up and down, as if wondering if we were likely to tamper with evidence. Then he plodded heavily to the squawk box. He fiddled with the switch, talked into it, then held his ear against the grate to listen. He needn't have worried about our overhearing. It's hard enough to figure out what's coming over those things when you've got your ear to them.

"Keep her down there," he said into the grille. "I'm on my way."

He released the switch and looked at us.

"We've got a preliminary," he said. "It's not definite, you understand, but it's a start. Dead four days. Arsenic poisoning."

SEVENTEEN

"It was the *manuscript,*" Caroline Dooley wailed. "All I wanted was the manuscript." She looked around the group of us in the lobby, partly furious, partly despairing. She must not have liked what she saw. Her face went red, her eyes dark.

"For God's sake," she said. "Somebody ripped up my office; I called looking for another copy of her *manuscript.* That's all."

"Somebody ripped up Sarah's manuscript?" I said.

"Somebody ripped up all the manuscripts," Caroline said. "Also the files, the scheduling sheets, the art notes—everything. Came in with a razor, according to the police." She gave the police a contemptuous glare. "Shredded the place. Even the carpet. If I didn't know where Dana Morton was at the time, I'd—"

"Why Dana Morton?" Tony Marsh said. "What does Dana Morton have against you?"

"Oh, don't be naive," Caroline said again. She stared at the pack of cigarettes I had taken out of my pocket, reached over, and took it from me. She lit up like a veteran. She threw the pack back to me and started blowing smoke rings. "You're not in the business," she said to Tony Marsh, "so I suppose I'll have to explain it to you. I'm putting out a line, a packaged series, of romantic suspense novels. So is Dana Morton."

"That should make you colleagues," Tony said.

"That should make us enemies," Caroline said, "and it would, except we have to do business when Dana's playing agent, so we stay polite. There's just so much room and no more in romantic suspense, and there are a lot of people out there with losses in straight romance trying to recoup. Writers under contract we can't get rid of because they have agents smart enough to take us to court. God only knows who ripped up my office, but whoever it was is doing romantic suspense and I tell you, I've had it. Just had it. I don't mind dog-eat-dog competition, I don't even mind out-and-out negotiating ruthlessness, but this is getting ridiculous. Somebody tried to hijack one of our trucks last month."

The truck was too much for Tony Marsh. He no longer looked confused. He looked obliterated.

"Somebody tried to hijack your truck," he repeated.

"Somebody tried to hijack one of our shipments. This isn't publishing anymore." She looked as if the enormity of it all had suddenly hit her. "This is *bootlegging.*" She gave me a wry look. "Just think how shocked we all were when *Fires of Love* turned out to be a scam," she said.

"I've got a copy of Sarah's manuscript," I said. "I'll send it over tomorrow."

"Make copies," Caroline said. She sighed. "This is going to set us back weeks. Maybe even months. And you know what that means."

Tony raised his eyebrows.

"Dana will get on the racks first," I explained. "That gives her an advantage."

"She already has an advantage," Caroline said. "Maybe she wouldn't have ripped up my office—I mean, God help us, what for? Everybody wants that line of hers, and those celebrity adventures. Written by and starring in, for God's sake. Marilou Saunders. That actress with the huge breasts and that television person who does the cat food commercials and—"

"I keep hearing about that," I said, "but I don't believe it. She must have got Marilou a ghost."

"No chance," Caroline said. "Gallard Rowson coughed up twenty thousand in advance for Marilou alone. Ten thousand for Verna. They have to write them themselves, it's part of the deal. Part of the selling strategy. First-person adventures by your favorite writers, actresses, pets—God only knows what. You know what Gallard Rowson is like. Literature. Honesty. Integrity. Horse manure."

"They'd rather put out the piece of excrement Marilou Saunders is going to write than a good book by a ghost?"

"That's what I hear."

"They're *crazy.*"

"Isn't everybody." Caroline dropped the butt end of her cigarette on the floor and ground it under her heel. Tony and Nick were staring at her, but they no longer made her nervous. She looked almost amused. "I really couldn't have started this thing, you know. I was in the Oyster Bar until we came up here in the cab, and by the time we got here the fire department was here. You can check."

Tony was solemn. "I'll check," he said. "I'll check carefully."

"You do that," Caroline stood up. "I'm going to check into a hotel." She looked at John Robert Train. "Or make other arrangements." She dismissed the rest of us with a wave. "Tomorrow I have to reconstruct my life *and* my work. Leave me alone."

EIGHTEEN

"Note for you on the chalkboard," Phoebe said when I came in. "I'll heat up the chicken."

I dumped my peacoat in the hall closet and wandered into the kitchen. Phoebe was perched on a chair at the kitchen table, romantic suspense posters and American Writers of Romance letterhead spread out before her. The chalkboard (ordered from Santini's, probably; it hadn't been in the kitchen when I left) said "Limo Will Pick You Up at 4 A.M.!!!" in green. I opened the refrigerator and rummaged through the neatly repackaged groceries—for some reason, Phoebe takes every item out of its wrapping as soon as she gets it home from the store and redoes it in Baggies and Saran Wrap—and found a decaffeinated Diet Coke. The Coke was sitting next to a twenty-pound turkey. I didn't have the faintest idea how to cook a twenty-pound turkey.

"What did you do with Nick's socks?" I asked her.

"I put them in a Baggie in the freezer," Phoebe said. "I put Adrienne to bed in your bed and I gave her a teddy bear I found in one of your closets. It's after twelve o'clock, McKenna."

"Got here as soon as I could." I took a kitchen chair and sat with my feet curled up under me, lotus fashion. It was just as well Adrienne was asleep. I was going to have to tell her her mother was dead one of these days, but I was in no hurry. I got the ashtray from the middle of the table and my cigarettes from my jacket pocket and looked at Phoebe's poster collection. "Dangerous Liaison," the top one said. A man and a woman stood on a narrow ledge on the face of an otherwise sheer cliff, embracing. Water rushed below them. Storm clouds raged above them. The woman was in an off-the-shoulder peasant blouse and four-inch high-heeled sandals.

"You want to see one of Dana's?" Phoebe asked. She pushed the poster to me. This one was called "Storm Warning." A man and a woman stood at the helm of a boat tossed in a bad sea, embracing. The deck was wet, the spray was half a foot over the side. The woman was in an off-the-shoulder peasant blouse and four-inch high-heeled sandals.

"We're doing a romance fair," Phoebe said. "At the conference. Conference time coming up again, you know." She smiled brightly, but without much hope. The only time I'd attended a romance conference, I'd been arrested for second-degree murder. I wasn't likely to go again.

"Let me tell you a story," I said. I gave her an outline of everything that had happened at Caroline's. It wasn't much, but it was more than Nick had told her. She nodded sagely throughout, looking like a bright little bird humoring a human who wants it to talk. Phoebe is curious but not intrusive. If I'd announced I was going to bed without telling her anything, she'd have forced a chicken breast and three potatoes down my throat and sent me off.

Now she pushed the American Writers of Romance letterhead away and said, "Am I crazy, or does none of this make any sense?"

"It makes a kind of sense," I said. "Somebody poisoned something in Dana's office, Halloween candy or coffee, still undecided. Maybe trying to kill Sarah, maybe trying to kill Marilou Saunders. I can think of two dozen people who'd like to kill Marilou Saunders."

"Marilou Saunders doesn't drink coffee," Phoebe said. "She says so all the time, even on television. And she can't eat candy and stay that thin."

"I can."

"You're abnormal. And Marilou Saunders isn't dead."

"Point taken. Somebody nearly killed me. Somebody killed Sarah, took her body out of Dana's reception room, hid it somewhere, dragged it up to Caroline's apartment—" I caught the look on Phoebe's face and shrugged. "Ridiculous, I know, but not impossible. She was a small woman. There are back entrances, back stairs."

"Somebody dragged that body through Dana's offices and out the service elevator?"

"Somebody had to. The police searched."

"Without Dana hearing it?"

"Maybe she was engaged at the time."

"Maybe she did it herself."

"She was there when 911 arrived," I shook my head. "She didn't have enough time to get the body out of the offices—off the floor—and get back to greet the ambulance. Not unless you people have the times messed up."

"The times," Phoebe said, "are part of the official record."

She got up to get the chicken out of the oven. Her bright yellow bathrobe flapped over her bare feet, making her look like a particularly exuberant monk. I wondered who had been doing errands for her—Nick? My super? Phoebe always manages to get people to do errands for her they wouldn't do for anyone else.

She put the chicken—enough to feed·the neighborhood—on a large dinner plate and brought it to me, together with fork, knife, soupspoon, and butter. I pushed it around and tried to decide if the idea of eating bothered me more than the idea of telling Phoebe I wouldn't.

Then I remembered something else.

"Did Amelia and Verna have a fight?"

Phoebe bit her lip and looked oddly un-Phoebe-like. "Why?" she asked me. "Did Amelia say something?"

"I haven't talked to Amelia. It's something this clerk in a bookstore said. Something she said she saw in *Romantic Times*. About Verna being kicked out of Farret and Amelia giving her a little push. Or something. I thought she must have got the story wrong. Amelia's a piss but she isn't usually vindictive. And she'll help people if they ask her to."

"I know what you mean," Phoebe said, "but not this time." She saw the surprise on my face and threw up her hands. "What am I going to tell you? It was about a year ago. There wasn't a fight, really. In fact, as far as I can tell, she and Verna were still friendly."

"But she wouldn't intervene with Farret?"

"She intervened with Farret," Phoebe said, "only she intervened to get Verna thrown out."

"But why?"

Phoebe shrugged. "Don't ask me," she said. "I'm just president of this organization. I tried to get Verna to bring a complaint with the AWR board, but she wouldn't do it. Said she and Amelia were working it out among themselves, I could stuff it, *et cetera*. So Farret cut her loose, Amelia invited her up to Rhinebeck for the weekend, and that was that."

"Anyone know what it's about?"

"No."

I stretched across the table and got the receiver from the wall phone. "Dial Amelia for me," I said.

"In Rhinebeck?"

"Of course in Rhinebeck."

The stiffness in Phoebe's back said she didn't think I'd be any more successful than she had been, but she dialed. There was always a chance Amelia would tell me *something*.

"It's the middle of the night," Amelia said when I finally got her on the line. Getting Amelia on the line meant going through three secretaries (all muddled), two connections, and five renditions of "Love Is a Many Splendored Thing." I considered complaining about this. I didn't.

"I'm taking a bath," Amelia said.

"I'm smoking a cigarette," I said. "I just wanted to ask you a question."

"You are interrupting my time with my Muse."

I lit a new cigarette with the butt of an old one and forcibly stopped myself from telling Amelia what I thought of that. Since the death of Myrra Agenworth, Amelia Samson had been the premier category romance writer in the United States. She hadn't actually written anything for twenty years. She had "secretaries." The "secretaries" got outlines and character sketches. The "secretaries" wrote the books. Amelia's formula being what it was, the "secretaries" had been writing the same book once a week since the system was put in operation.

It has always been my opinion that Amelia's Muse quotes the Dow Jones.

"Phoebe said you had a fight with Verna," I said.

There was a pause on the other end of the line. "I didn't have a *fight* with Verna," Amelia said. "We were always on amiable terms."

"So you had her kicked out of Farret?"

"I didn't," Amelia stopped. She took a deep breath. I could hear the sound of ice in a glass in the background. "Why," she said, "do you want to know about Verna?"

I considered possible answers to this. The truth was simple—I wanted to know because the story didn't make sense, because I was curious, because I can't stand not knowing what is going on. The truth was going to get nowhere with Amelia. Dramatics might.

"Verna is dead," I said virtuously. "Somebody tried to kill me."

There was a background sound of ice in a gin glass, a deep breath that meant Amelia was taking a drag of a Secret Cigarette. Amelia smoked only Secret Cigarettes. No fan ever saw her with a butt in her hand.

"Nobody killed Verna," Amelia said positively.

"Are you going to deny someone tried to kill me?"

"A maniac."

I chalked one up for the grapevine. Every romance writer, mystery writer, agent, and editor in New York probably already knew more about my illness than I did.

"They found Sarah English's body today," I said. "She'd been dead four days. They found her in Caroline's apartment. Verna's dead, Amelia. All I want to know—"

"I can't tell you over the phone."

"Amelia, I'm sick, for God's sake. I can't go hauling out to Rhinebeck."

"The Russian Tea Room," Amelia said.

"Now?"

"I'll make reservations for lunch at one." Another pause. "If you're pulling some kind of shit," she said, "I'll poison your soup myself."

She hung up.

I handed the receiver to Phoebe.

"Lunch at the Russian Tea Room," I said. "Everybody else goes to Le Cirque, Amelia goes to the Russian Tea Room."

"She's going to tell you what happened?"

"She didn't exactly say."

"If she tells you, tell me," Phoebe said. "I've got an open file at AWR."

"Right," I said. I pushed the chicken and potatoes away and got up, stretching. It had not been the most sensible first day out of the hospital. If Nick hadn't gone home to his apartment for the first time in three months, he would have lectured me. I was surprised he hadn't called to lecture me on the phone.

"Television tomorrow," Phoebe said, waving at the chalk-board.

"Four o'clock in the morning," I said. "That's why Marilou takes drugs. She has to get up at four o'clock in the morning."

"I'm going to take Adrienne out and buy her a television," Phoebe said. "Speaking of television, she tells me she's never had one."

I nodded wearily, heading for the living room. Halfway to the hall, I stopped, bothered. Someone had said something that didn't make sense. Phoebe had said something that didn't make sense. Worse, it made the opposite of sense. I tried to remember what it was, but couldn't. I gave it up. Whatever it was, it couldn't be important enough to keep me from sleep.

Adrienne was lying at the edge of the far side of my bed, one arm around a teddy bear and the other around Camille. Phoebe had wrapped Adienne's braids into a crown on the top of her head, to make it easier for her to sleep.

I put on a pair of pajamas and got in the empty side, surprised at how little space children occupy in the material universe.

NINETEEN

I found the little silver thing in the pocket of my dress when I reached for cigarettes. It had been on my bedside table, and so had the cigarettes, so I figured I must have swept the whole mess into my pocket without looking on my way out the door that morning. I lay the little silver thing in the palm of one hand and prodded it with the fingers of the other, trying to decide what it was. Then a disembodied voice above my head said, "Miss Mc-Kenna, you're ruining my concentration," and I had to put it back in my pocket.

I was in Makeup. The disembodied voice above my head belonged to Angelo, who was a one-man crusade for the Preservation of Gay Culture. Angelo had three earrings in his left ear, four handkerchiefs stuffed so tightly down the front of his jeans they creased when he inhaled, an electric blue satin shirt, and mink eyelashes. I was all but strapped into a hydraulic dentist's chair with black plastic upholstered seats and mysterious chrome torture instruments welded to the frame. A great many arc lights were trained on a point a little to the left of my nose. It was quarter after five in the morning.

The Network had sent a stretch limousine for me, complete with uniformed driver guaranteed to be deaf. The driver has to be deaf or he'd hear what the Guest says about the Network for forcing the Guest out of bed at this hour of the morning. He has to be uniformed to make muggers think he's a cop. Muggers generally being drug addicts, this is not entirely impossible. My driver held the door for me, showed me the location of coffee and cigarettes (built into an imitation NASA Central that popped out of the back of the driver's seat), and asked me if I wanted to watch television. The television came out of a trap door in the roof on a crane. I could also make phone calls. I started doing some serious smoking.

I intended to catch Marilou Saunders as soon as I walked in the door. I had a crazy idea I could lock her in her dressing room and force her to talk by threatening to read her something. It wasn't possible. She was there. She came sweeping into her dressing room surrounded by a multitude of little old ladies in gray cotton smocks embroidered with the Network logo, looking like a junkie after four weeks of good luck. The little old ladies formed a barrier. The door to her dressing room was locked. Miss Saunders was Unavailable until Air Time. By the time Air Time came around, I was imprisoned in the chair.

"Did you see that thing I was holding?" I asked Angelo.

"I can see the pores in your face," Angelo said. "If you don't shut up, everybody in America will see the pores in your face."

"They'll love the pores in my face," I said. I got the little silver thing out of my pocket. "Look at this. Do you know what it is?"

"You're ruining your lip line."

"Give me the lip line I've always had. I like it."

"Nobody else does."

"What is this thing?"

Angelo gave an exaggerated sigh, bent over my palm, and closed one eye like a jeweler looking through a magnifying piece. He straightened almost instantly.

"It's a little silver thing," he said.

I almost asked him if he knew Phoebe Damereaux. I didn't, because he probably did. Phoebe had appeared on "Wake Up and Shine" more often than I'd want to count. I wasn't ready for a lecture on how he wished everybody could be as cooperative as Miss Damereaux. People are always giving me lectures about how everybody should be as cooperative as Miss Damereaux.

"You're going to need all the help you can get," Angelo said.

"There's nothing wrong with my face."

"I'm not worried about your face. I'm worried about *her.*" He swiveled a hip in the direction I took to be toward the set and smirked. "It's bad enough she can't read. It's bad enough she won't listen to the tapes they give her with the synopses of the books on them. Today she's still high from last night."

"Oh, fine."

"And she doesn't like you much, either. Tried to get you thrown off the schedule. Not that that makes you anything unusual with her, if you know what I mean."

"Austin, Stoddard & Trapp owns the Network."

"The Network owns Austin, Stoddard & Trapp."

"Same difference."

"Possibly she got enough speed into herself to stand up straight," Angelo said. "Or they got enough speed into her. She's a puddle."

"How does that woman get anything done?" I asked him. "She runs an interview show. She's written a book—"

"Written a book? She uses books for coasters. She thinks books are bound toilet tissue."

"That's what I said," I told him, "but someone who should know says she's actually written a book. It doesn't change what I said about the show. When does she get off that stuff long enough to do the show?"

Angelo smirked again, letting me see his dimple. "She doesn't run the show," he said. "The show runs her. She shows up for the show. The show feeds her intravenously. She's colorful, you see."

"She still has to go on, for God's sake."

"She's propped up in her chair. Once she gets in front of the camera, she goes on automatic pilot. It doesn't matter how outrageous she is. She's supposed to be outrageous. That sells the show."

"To whom?"

"The Network will do anything for her," Angelo said. "She's the first thing with decent ratings against that cheerleader at NBC. The Network will do *anything.*" He pursed his lips. For the first time, I realized he was wearing lipstick. Dimestore Vermilion Passion lipstick. "Well," he conceded, "not anything."

"They won't buy her drugs for her," I said.

"Oh, they'd do that if they had to." Angelo gave me a limp

wrist. He was very proud of his limp wrist. "Fortunately, Ms. Saunders has her own connections in that regard. What they won't give her is an alibi."

"Alibi?"

"Some bimbo says our dear Ms. Saunders was hanging around when she—the bimbo—got poisoned, and apparently she was, or she doesn't remember, which is more likely, but anyway, they won't do it for her. They'll make sure nobody talks to her, but they won't lie to the police for her." He gave me his dimple again. "I won't do it either," he said.

I was very, very cautious. Even through terminal fatigue, I knew how important this was. "She asked you to give her an alibi for a time someone was poisoned?"

"She asked everybody," Angelo said. "She asked the night clerk, and he isn't even here in the middle of the afternoon—the alibi time, sweetheart."

A red light stuck in the wall over the mirror started to flash. Angelo made agitated stabs at my eyelids with what looked like a surgical instrument.

"That's two minutes," he said. "You have to get moving."

Under other circumstances, I might have behaved myself. Being on television frightens me. I don't have that much to say. What I do have to say is probably actionable. I am also overly aware that anything I say is going to be heard by my mother. No matter what my mother says in public, she is very careful to watch every show I'm on and read every word I've written.

This time I was too angry to care. I kept seeing the faces of Tony Marsh, and Nick, and even Phoebe when I told them Marilou and Sarah had been in that room. That, more than the fact that someone had killed Sarah and nearly killed me, fueled my rage. I heard my name called over a loudspeaker. I felt the clammy hand of a production assistant on my back. I saw a light go on over the curtained entrance to the set. The next thing I knew, I was trying to walk sideways across the stage while smiling directly at the camera with the light on over it.

Marilou Saunders was sprawled in a paisley wingback chair,

hands folded in her lap, legs crossed at the knee, eyebrows arched. She was wearing a yellow peekaboo blouse just this side of legal and a skirt so straight it looked poured in concrete. Behind her was a publicity poster for her romantic suspense novel and a minidump of advance copies. The painting showed a man and a woman climbing a rope over a plunging canyon, woman first, man bringing up the rear and kissing her ankle passionately in the process. The woman was wearing an off-the-shoulder peasant blouse and four-inch high-heeled sandals. I took one of the books and stuffed it into my pocket.

"Patience!" Marilou said deliriously as I sat in the wingback opposite her. She snatched a copy of *my* book from the desk and held it in the air, backward, so my picture was showing. This let her audience know I had written a book without making them feel they knew enough about it to have to go out and buy it.

Marilou turned to the camera. "Well!" she said, leaving the country of delirium for the realm of orgasm. "We've been reading about you in the papers again, haven't we? I believe the New York *Post* even had your—obituary?" She gave this last a broad interpretation and a wink. I had a sudden vision of her announcing the starvation toll in Ethiopia with a giggle. It was awesome to contemplate.

"Well!" Marilou gasped again. "You're not dead, are you?"

You couldn't have held me down with cast-iron constraints: Marilou's face worked like a mechanical doll's with a nervous tic. She had a copy of the *Post* by her chair. She was grinning at me.

"You certainly don't look dead," she trilled.

"No thanks to you," I said.

The smile never faltered. The eyes never stopped rolling. The words, however, were mangled. Marilou Saunders croaked.

"You had to just leave me there?" I asked her. "You couldn't have waited for the ambulance? And what about *Sarah?*"

"We're on the *air,*" Marilou hissed. The hissing was new. Nothing else was. Eyes continued to roll, smile continued to proclaim sunshine and light for the world. "You can't *do* this."

"They found Sarah's body yesterday," I said. "She'd been dead for four days. She must have been dead when you *left.*"

Jerky little hand signals were added to the rolling eyes and the smile. "I'm going to have your *ass.*"

"Oh, Jesus Christ," someone in the back said. "We were broadcasting. That went *out.* What's the matter with that asshole in the booth?"

"You just said asshole on a nationwide hookup," somebody else said.

"Why don't we break for a commercial?" Marilou giggled.

Nothing happened. *Nothing happened.* The same lights continued blinking on the same cameras. The same cameramen continued to point the same cameras in our direction. They could only hear the director in the booth, not us, but by then even I thought the director should have intervened.

Marilou staggered to her feet. "You *bastard,*" she screamed in the direction of the control booth. "You've always been after my ass, you goddamned self-righteous son of a *bitch—*"

All the lights in the studio went out.

Marilou looked around the darkened set, blinked, and threw herself into her wingback. "You bitch," she said to me. "The two of you had it planned. That black bastard has had it in for me from the beginning, the Christ-damned stuck-up son of a whore, and this time you were in on it, goddamn you."

"I was in on what?" I said. "You're the one running around refusing to talk to people. You're the one who said you were never there, which you were, because I saw you there, and how do I know you didn't kill Sarah and put her body in Caroline's apartment?"

"That's slander," Marilou said. "I can sue you for slander and I'm going to sue you for slander and if they take me off the air I'm going to sue you for more than that, you and that black son of a bitch who calls himself a television director."

"Sarah English is dead," I shouted. "Where did you go? What do you think you're trying to get away with? If you didn't do anything, why are you hiding?"

"Who the screwing frog do you think you are?"

The "screwing frog" activated something in the back. We were suddenly surrounded by people. Two nervous young men with bantamweight builds pulled at Marilou's arms, trying to drag her into the wings. Nobody touched me—in heels I'm almost six three, and can look formidable—but I was cordoned off by people. It made me laugh. They'd used their heavies for me, but I was the one willing to go. Marilou was taking her two bodyguards apart.

"I'll tell you now what I told you then," she screamed at me. "I'm not going to let that little bitch drag me into her crap, not for any price, do you hear me?"

"What little bitch?" I screamed back. "Who are you talking about?"

She broke away from the bantamweights and came at me—fast. My bodyguards didn't have a chance to reaet. She had her nails into the silk of my shirtwaist before anyone even knew she was moving. She had ripped the right lapel from the dress front before they had a chance to get to her.

"I know what you're doing," she hissed at me, "and I'm not having any, McKenna. *I'm not having any.* You can take that home and stuff it where the sun don't shine and then you can tell *her.*"

This time two of the biggest ones got a grip on her.

TWENTY

I had to go home to change my dress. The Network offered to buy me another—take the dress size, send someone to Saks, deliver an identical replacement—but it would have taken too long. I wanted some peace and quiet before I met Amelia. My refusal made the fat little emissary from middle management very unhappy. I might hold the Network responsible. I might sue.

"Of course Miss Saunders wasn't herself today," the emissary said. "You have to excuse Miss Saunders."

"Miss Saunders was as much herself as I've ever seen her," I said. "You ought to put a leash on that woman."

"Of course, if she knows anything about a crime, I'm sure she'd be happy to testify," the emissary said. "Our understanding, though, is that—"

"She doesn't have to testify," I said, "just talk to the police. And I don't care what your understanding is. I was there. So was she."

"Ah," the emissary said. "Well. We will of course talk to Miss Saunders about that. In fact, someone is talking to Miss Saunders about that right now. However—"

I dismissed him. I knew what "however" meant. I also knew Marilou could no longer get away with it. My story was becoming more plausible by the minute. Hers was beginning to look sick. Tony Marsh had his body.

I refused the offer of a limousine and took a cab to the West Side, feeling very high. I thought I finally had a handle on this thing. I felt in control of it. I thought I knew how to approach it.

I ran into my apartment, hot to tell Phoebe all about it, and found a note on the kitchen table. "Have taken Adrienne to Eeyore's," it said. Eeyore's is a children's bookstore. I crumpled the note into a ball and threw it into the yellow plastic garbage pail Phoebe had acquired while I was out. I considered going to Eeyore's to find them. I rejected the idea. As far as I knew, Adrienne did not yet know her mother was dead. Talking to Adrienne about Sarah dying was going to take all afternoon whenever I did it. It might take several days. I couldn't break that up to have lunch with Amelia.

I called Nick's office. His secretary answered, murmured gracious hellos, and said Nick was in conference. The conference wasn't going anywhere. If I got in a cab right this minute, Nick would be ready to see me when I arrived.

I changed into a skirt and sweater and flat-heeled boots and headed for the door.

Nick's office is in the far West Forties, in one of those buildings that look designed to house novelty companies and porno publishers on their way to bankruptcy. In the beginning, when Nick had just left Nader's Raiders and his partner had just escaped from a white-shoe Wall Street firm, the address had been functional. The rent was minimal for Manhattan. Now that Nick and David were doing well, they were reluctant to move. Their clients like coming to Eleventh Avenue. Eleventh Avenue had atmosphere. Eleventh Avenue showed that Life was Real and Life was Earnest. Since most of their clients were either romance writers or small romance packagers, this was supposed to make sense.

It did not make sense to me. I had lived in terrible buildings in terrible neighborhoods when I was working cheap. To my mind, you worked, you advanced, and you moved into something more comfortable. Preferably on Columbus Avenue in the Seventies.

I had to ring six buzzers before someone let me into the lobby. I had to ring six more buzzers before the elevator door opened. The owners and occupants obviously thought a surfeit of buzzers would defeat the average mugger, who was reputed to be too stupid to count and too strung out to remember anything from one second to the next.

I had to stand under a prism viewer before Nick's secretary let me into the office. She came to the door and opened it for me. She didn't want me to get the idea she had anything against me personally.

"He's in the back by himself," she said, closing the door behind me. "As soon as I said you were coming over, he locked himself in his office with a lot of papers."

"I'll talk him out of it," I said.

I plowed into the back and barged into Nick's office without knocking. I was expected. Like all secretaries, Nick's called ahead.

I dropped into his client's chair, the one that his mother had bought for her first apartment. In 1948. "I wanted to talk to somebody," I said. "I think I have something worked out. I wanted you to look at it."

"Why me? Why not Phoebe?" He ran a hand through his hair. "That's what usually happens around here. You and Phoebe get into trouble, as much trouble as you can think of, and then as soon as you're arrested or somebody ties you up in a closet, I'm supposed to be the cavalry and rescue you."

"Phoebe took Adrienne to Eeyore's," I said.

"You don't want to talk to Adrienne about Sarah," Nick said.

"I'll get around to it," I said.

He pushed the papers on his desk a little farther toward the center and tipped his swivel chair toward the wall. He looked exhausted and none too happy with me. I expected another lecture. Instead, he said, "Tell me your beautiful solution." He said it the way an overtried father would tell his prodigal son, "Give me the excuse this time."

I hesitated. I decided I was being silly. Nick is always like that, in the beginning. "It's not a solution," I told him. "It's a problem. I worked out a chain of events—" I stopped. I threw out an empty Merit box and extracted a fresh one from my bag. "You remember the night Sarah arrived and you told me about Dana's suspense line and you said she had her ass to the wind?" I said. "That's not what I hear from everybody else. What I hear from everybody else is the idea's going like wildfire."

"If it is, then she doesn't have her ass to the wind anymore."

"Right," I said.

Nick shrugged. "I told you what the projections were. Maybe they were wrong. If they were wrong, Gallard Rowson is going to make a lot of money. So is Dana."

"Could they be that wrong?"

He grinned. "Remember Farret Paperback Originals?" he said. "Of course they could be that wrong. This is a more pleasant way to be wrong. Maybe the books aren't as bad as everybody thought they would be. Maybe celebrity names are enough."

"Mmm," I said. I had a copy of Marilou's book in my bag. I had a terrible feeling I ought to read it.

"Tell me about your timetable," Nick said.

I took a blank piece of paper from his desk and a pen from his pencil holder. I wrote "Sequence" at the top of the page.

"First," I said, "Verna dies. That's Thursday night, Friday morning. Don't frown at me like that. First, Verna dies. Then Sarah dies. I'm poisoned. Marilou is in Dana's reception room and says she isn't. Caroline's office gets ripped up. You see anything wrong with that?"

"I don't see what Verna has to do with it."

"I don't see how anyone could have both poisoned that coffee *and* ripped up Caroline's office," I said.

"Halloween candy," Nick said.

"I don't care what it was in. The timing is still wrong. That was lunch hour. Caroline's office is halfway across town from Dana's. Nobody could have done both those things."

"Maybe nobody did." Nick put his head in his hands. "McKenna, you still can't prove the poisoning was deliberate. Okay, somebody moved Sarah's body. Maybe Marilou Saunders did it to avoid the scandal."

"Maybe I have green hair. Nick—"

"Answer a question for me," Nick said. "What for?"

"You've been saying that for days."

"I have to say it. One of two things has to be true. Either everything that's happened has been a deliberate plan, at which point you have to decide why anyone would want to kill a second-rate romance writer and a hick from Connecticut. Or only some of it was deliberate, which leaves you a lot less to explain."

"Just who moved Sarah's body. And why."

"Exactly. Marilou Saunders. To keep her name out of the papers. To give herself a chance to disassociate herself from the poisoning. By the time she found out it was caused by a nut, she'd have to go through with getting rid of Sarah's body anyway, because she had Sarah's body."

"So she put it in Caroline Dooley's apartment and lit a match?"

"Marilou Saunders?" Nick said. "Why not? Didn't I just see her throwing a temper tantrum full of four-letter words on national television?"

I blushed. "It wasn't my fault," I said.

"You started it," he said.

"It may be the simplest explanation, but it doesn't solve anything," I said. "It doesn't explain why no one was poisoned by the candy before—"

"Luck."

"And Verna—"

"An accident."

"And all the phone calls saying it was Sarah—"

"Marilou covering her ass."

"Explain someone ripping up Caroline's office and taking her keys," I said. I sounded sullen.

"Romance sabotage, of which there's been quite a bit recently. Nothing so blatant as that, mind you, but quite a bit. And we don't really know someone took Caroline's keys. Caroline lost her keys, from what Tony Marsh tells me, the same day her office was torn apart. The super got her a new set made. Okay. But there's nothing to say it's connected. She's a bubble head. She'd lose her rear end if it wasn't screwed on."

"That's a mess," I said.

"Okay," he said. "So tell me, first, why someone would want to kill Verna and Sarah? And while you're at it, think up a plot for a conspiracy, because you're right. If someone was trying to kill you, or Sarah, or Marilou, deliberately, then that person could not also have ripped up Caroline's office. Not unless he had a helicopter at his disposal."

"I didn't know that part about Caroline and the keys," I said. "Not all of it."

He gave me an evil look. "It's not always a mystery, McKenna. Sometimes it's just a lot of bad luck. And coincidences happen."

"Horse manure," I said. I started to gather up my things. "With you, it's *never* a mystery."

"This is the woman," he said, "who less than a week ago said she only wanted to deal with *ancient* murders. Ancient history."

"The key," I said, "is finding out how those two things could have been done at once. That's the key."

Nick just shook his head.

TWENTY-ONE

Amelia got to the Russian Tea Room before I did. Got there and set up shop. Although knowledgeable New Yorkers refuse to sit "upstairs," Amelia *preferred* upstairs. There was more room to spread out. Amelia at lunch needed a lot of room to spread out. By the time I was shown to her table, she had territorialized the entire west corner of the room. It was quarter after one. She was dressed in vintage Worth and had an ostrich feather in her hair.

"It's always such an *experience* having her with us," the hostess said, bringing me upstairs. "Miss Samson is a very loyal customer."

A waiter took over at the top of the stairs, showed me to my seat (the only one of six at Amelia's table not covered with papers), held my chair, and promised to come back immediately with "another cocktail for Miss Samson." Miss Samson already had a cocktail. It was pink. It had red and green and blue flags in it.

"I suppose it also has gin in it," I said, stowing my tote bag at my feet. "Do you have to do that in the middle of the afternoon?"

"Gin and grenadine," Amelia said. "Doesn't it look awful? If anybody asks, I can always say it's a Shirley Temple."

"Will anybody believe it?"

"Fans believe it. Fans"—she shook her head resentfully—"are the only problem with the Russian Tea Room."

I didn't tell her she'd have less trouble with fans if she stopped sending her heroines to dinner in her favorite restaurants. The waiter came back with another cocktail and the menus. We ordered a pair of chicken Kievs and waved the man away.

I got a cigarette out and lit it. "This ought to be good," I said. "You couldn't just tell me over the phone?"

"My phone has been tapped for years," Amelia said. "Besides, this isn't a publishing place." She patted the nearest stack of papers. "I don't leave these lying around, you know."

I picked up the stack closest to me. It was a typed plot outline for a book called *Into His Arms,* in which a shy, sensitive seventeen-year-old is forced by the deaths of both her parents to leave the protective confines of her convent school in Yorkshire (a convent school in Yorkshire?) to become governess to the children of infamous industrialist Black Jack Marlowe. I reached across the table for the stack of papers marked "scene." *Into His Arms* took place in the winter of 1981–82. I put the stack of papers back.

"Seems right on the mark," I said blandly.

Amelia snorted. "Oh, I know what you think of this sort of thing. I know what all of you think. The brave new world of sex and the executive woman and fifty-fifty marriages." She waved her gin in the air. "Asinine. Falling on your heads. To be expected."

"I don't write romances any more," I said. "Phoebe has executive women, or the historical equivalent. She does very well."

"Your Miss Damereaux is a very smart woman," Amelia said. "I've never said otherwise."

Amelia had not only said otherwise, she had once implied that both Phoebe and I were fourth-rate human beings bent on destroying her. At the time, she had lifted me off my feet by the front of my sweater and was slamming me into a tile wall in a utility room in the Cathay Pierce Hotel. Amelia Samson is fat, but the bulk in her shoulders is all muscle, and she knows how to use it. I opted for discretion and sat quietly while the waiter brought single (for me) and double (for Amelia) chicken Kievs.

When he was gone, Amelia did the unexpected. She ignored her lunch. She reached into her bag and came up with a book.

"Look at this," she handed it over.

It was a Dortman & Hodges paperback of Verna's last "big" contemporary, *Flight into Romance.* I could tell it was romance and not romantic suspense because although the heroine was fleeing for her life down a forest path, she was in *Cosmopolitan* lingerie instead of an off-the-shoulder peasant blouse.

I turned the book over and read the jacket copy. It was the story of a shy and sensitive seventeen-year-old who is forced by the deaths of both her parents to leave the protective confines of her convent school in Milwaukee to become governess to the children of the infamous industrialist Black Jack Harrow.

I put the book down next to my soupspoon. I was starving, but I couldn't have put food in my mouth if my life depended on it.

"I don't understand," I said.

Amelia was attacking her lunch. "What's to understand? She ripped me off."

"How could she have ripped you off?" I asked her. "Her book's already in print. Yours is just an outline."

"My book has been an outline since two years ago last Christmas," Amelia said. "I've got a room full of outlines back home. For God's sake, you know what I have to produce in a month. What if I got sick? I have to have inventory."

"Inventory," I said.

"I've got a file cabinet full of manila envelopes sealed by a notary," Amelia said. "I always make sure one of my girls is a notary. I keep the file *locked.*"

"Then how did Verna get hold of this?"

Amelia waved the fork. "Those aren't the only copies. I've got copies all over the house. Those are just to protect me."

"Oh," I said.

"My heroine's name is Susannah Place," Amelia said. "Hers is Susannah Parrish."

"But *Amelia,*" I said.

"But Amelia nothing. She paid one of my girls and got the outline and used it. I'm not guessing, Patience. She told me. The girl told me, too, after I confronted her. Paid her five thousand dollars. Verna did."

"Dear Lord."

"Fired the girl. Came to an agreement with Verna."

"That's why she wouldn't file a complaint with AWR," I said. "That's been driving Phoebe crazy."

"If it had really been driving Phoebe crazy, she'd have done something about it," Amelia said. "Like I said, she's a smart woman. She knew something was screwy. And what was I supposed to do? I couldn't just let it go."

No, I thought, she couldn't just let it go. The old ladies of romance were nobody's fools. Their books might be treacle, but their heads were solid rock. They could forgive you any personal betrayal. They would drop a forty-year friendship in a minute for any *business* betrayal. I was surprised Amelia hadn't exposed Verna and had done with it.

"The real problem in a case like this," Amelia said, "is you know how it happened and you don't want to make it worse. Also, you don't want to give *them*"—romance writers routinely refer to all nonromance writers, especially members of what they think of as the Literary Establishment (such as Sidney Sheldon), as *them*—"a chance to make fun of us. And with everything falling apart the way it is—"

"But why would she *do* something like this?" I said. "Even if I grant her career was going nowhere, and no matter what else I think of what you do, I know you've done better than this—"

"Of course I've done better than this," Amelia said. "What do you take me for?"

"Then why steal it in the first place? It wouldn't have advanced her career. It wasn't her kind of thing."

"It would have ruined her career if she'd started reneging on contracts. Which she almost did."

I bit my lip. One of the iron rules of romance publishing is that you never fail to deliver a book when you promise one. The lines run more like magazines than book publishers. They put out a certain number of books each month. Their lead time gives them very little room to establish inventory. Even "big" romances are produced on a schedule designed to give the world's most ardent workaholic a nervous breakdown. To renege on a contract, unless you were an Amelia or a Phoebe, might easily mean you never worked again.

"She had writer's block," I said slowly.

"Bullshit," Amelia said. "She had burnout. The last three

books before this and the two after were written by what's his name. The objectionable asshole with the pornographic mystery titles."

"Max Brady?" I had forgotten Max Brady.

"Max Brady," Amelia said. "My feeling is, he wrote every one in the last two years except the one she took from me and this new one. God only knows who wrote the new one. It wasn't Verna."

"How can you be sure?"

"Wait till it comes out," Amelia said.

"I don't think she's supposed to be able to do that. Get a ghost, I mean. From what I hear, for Dana's line, even Marilou Saunders had to write her own."

"Maybe she didn't tell Dana."

"It's supposed to be great romantic suspense," I said. "Not just okay. Great. Why would somebody do something like that and not publish it on her own?"

Amelia shrugged again. "Don't know and don't care. I read it. It's good for that kind of thing. And Verna didn't write it. Believe me." She finished her drink in a single long swallow. "The way Verna was going, she was turning into a house name."

It went through me like an electric shock.

"What?" I said. "What did you say?"

"I didn't say anything," Amelia said. "I want another drink. Sit down and have your lunch."

"House names," I said. "Ellery Queen. Everything is going to make sense."

Amelia thought I was out of my mind, but I didn't care. What had Phoebe said? "She was saying something about Ellery Queen being a lot of people." Right. I crammed things into my tote bag, dropping them in my hurry. I had to get Max Brady. I had to get to him right away.

I didn't know why Sarah had died, but I thought I knew why Verna had. If I was right, maybe Nick had been half right.

Maybe it was Marilou someone had meant to kill.

Amelia waved her fork at me. "So I'll eat your lunch," she said. "You've always been a crazy person."

TWENTY-TWO

I wanted to go directly to Max Brady's. Instead, I made myself detour to the 42nd Street Library magazine room—just to be sure. I read ten books and two dozen magazines a month. I could have been confused. If I *was* confused, my whole theory was a piece of nonsense.

I wasn't confused. It took me a while to find what I was looking for—I thought the article had appeared in *The Armchair Detective;* it was in the March issue of *Gumshoes* instead—but when I did, it was exactly as I had remembered it. The title, banally enough, was "Will the Real Ellery Queen Please Stand Up?" The byline read, "Additional Research by Max Brady." I tapped my finger against the "Max Brady." That was better than I could have hoped.

The theory went like this: Not all Ellery Queen books were written by Ellery Queen (Frederic Dannay and Manfred B. Lee, or Frederic Dannay and whomever after Lee died). Some of them were written by rank outsiders and did not feature Queen as a detective. They were published as "by Ellery Queen" because books "by Ellery Queen" made more money than books by other mystery writers. It was a weird situation. Most house names are invented by the publishing company. Superfantastic Books thinks it could make a lot of money with a series about a mercenary soldier. Marketing and editorial get together and invent a name for our hero ("Cannonball Jones") and a name for the writer ("Mack Savage"). They then go out and hire a lot of writers to produce books that will be published as "by Mack Savage." The writers get no credit, minimal royalties, and a minuscule advance. The "Ellery Queen" setup was the only one anyone had heard of that involved the name of an actual, living writer being farmed out with the writer's permission. Assuming Dannay and Lee had given their permission. Assuming such a situation had ever actually existed. No one was absolutely sure, and Dannay and Lee were now both dead.

I put the magazine back in its filing box. It was the only thing that made sense of the "Ellery Queen" conversation Phoebe had reported to me. I wondered what Max had told Verna. Ellery Queen did it, so it was all right if she did it? Gallard Rowson was being stuffy with all their "truth in advertising" bull? He had written a book for Marilou, so there was no reason he shouldn't write another for her? By the time Verna got around to stealing Amelia's pitiful excuse for an outline, she must have been desperate. She would probably have listened to anything.

Max Brady had an even greater need for money than Verna. He had an ex-wife who liked to keep tabs on him. From all indications, his career as the hopeful successor to Hammett and Chandler was a dismal failure.

I took the box back to the checkout desk and headed out of the library. For all I knew, Max was ghosting half the romantic suspense books in town. He couldn't let anyone know. It would finish him in the mystery writers' community. They would forgive him Melissa Crowell—everybody has money problems now and then—but consorting with those "romantic suspense bimbos" would be something else.

Suddenly, I had *exactly the solution I wanted* all tied up with a ribbon.

Max Brady lived in a fifth-floor walk-up in a decaying brownstone surrounded by abandoned tenements on Thirty-ninth Street off Tenth Avenue. A little further east, the area was beginning to have a certain vogue. The residents had renamed it Clinton and gone public in *New York* magazine on the joys of ethnicity. Max's block was still recognizable as Hell's Kitchen.

I walked into his vestibule and stared apprehensively at the double line of mailboxes just outside the inner door. The mailboxes had buzzer buttons incorporated in them. Most of the

buzzer buttons were broken. So was the lock on the inner door. I
pressed Max's buzzer and waited. Nothing happened.

I pushed the inner door. It creaked forward, revealing a cement block floor carpeted with four-letter words and girls' names
(with phone numbers). I hesitated.

It would have been easier if I'd wanted Max to be home. I
wanted to break into his apartment. With any luck, the manuscript of Marilou's book would be on his desk and a box of rat
poison under his kitchen sink.

I swallowed my conscience and headed up the stairs. All
brownstones built in a certain era for people of modest means
have the same stairs—metal-railed, narrow, slippery with lino-
leum. All of them have the same light fixtures in the stairwells,
big square fluorescents more often out than on. Only one of the
fluorescents in Max's stairwell was on, the one on the second-
floor landing. As soon as I got beyond it, I was in darkness.

I had to count landings to know where I was. It was impossible
to see apartment numbers on doors. According to Max's
mailbox, he lived in 5E. I got to the fifth-floor landing and looked
around. There were only two apartment doors.

I stood in the darkness and listened. After a while, I heard a
sound from the front apartment, an out-of-key voice doing oper-
atic scales. The voice was so off-key, it could have cut through
the building supports and brought the house down.

I went to the door of the back apartment. I pressed the buzzer.
I waited. Nothing happened. Either Max was out, or he was
passed out. If he was passed out, he might or might not wake up
when I broke in on him.

I have had some experience with murderers. They are not safe
people to know. They are certainly not the kind of people you
want to stumble over while obviously checking into their affairs.
I am not a cautious woman, but I have a reasonable amount of
common sense. I have no interest in getting myself killed. On the
other hand, Max Brady drunk and passed out, or drunk and
awakening from a hangover, was hardly a figure of fear I could
take seriously. Max Brady sober was hardly a figure of fear I

could take seriously. He was simply too small and too out of shape.

I got out my credit cards, then dismissed them for my driver's license. For some reason, I keep my Connecticut driver's license. It is laminated in plastic. It is very thin. It is perfect for doors.

I had a moment of worry that Max might have been sensible enough to get himself a dead bolt. I couldn't get past a dead bolt with my driver's license. *Phoebe* had trouble getting past dead bolts, and Phoebe can open any lock ever made just by looking at it. I put my license in the crack and drew it upward.

This is the kind of thing you learn by reading too many detective stories.

The lock creaked, whined, and popped. The door swung open on the most god-awful mess I'd ever seen.

I almost didn't have the courage to enter. There were massive black plastic garbage bags, full of now-returnable beer and soda cans, covering the kitchen floor. There were piles of takeout cartons (mostly Chinese and pizza) covering the kitchen table. Turning sideways toward the single room, I saw three months' worth of laundry in piles on the floor, four-months-in-use sheets on the unmade bed, and a congealed hot turkey sandwich plate (half-eaten) on the night table. The only thing that made the room less depressing than Cassie Arbeth's house was the worktable by the window. The worktable was pristine. The typewriter was not only new, it looked dusted. Typewriter paper was stacked neatly in boxes. Even the work in progress had a small open box of its own, placed just to the right of the keyboard.

If Max was anywhere in that room, he was buried for the duration. I let the door swing closed behind me, peeked into the bathroom just to make sure, and then headed for the worktable. I did not have to search the apartment. If Max was getting paid for it, it was laid out neatly and efficiently among all the other things he was getting paid for.

I could deal with the kitchen—and possible sources of arsenic —later.

I stepped over a pile of ancient, torn, reeking T-shirts and looked at the page in the typewriter. The work in progress was a novel called *Roses for the Reaper*. Brady was writing it under his own name. Page 106 started:

> There are too many scum like Halloran in the best society. What honest crooks and tenth-rate con-men are jailed for without benefit of clergy, the Hallorans of this world expect to get handed to them on a platter. What Halloran wanted handed to him on a platter this time was my head. I wasn't going to give it to him.

I went around this paragraph a few times, then gave up on it. I was sure it made something like sense to Brady and his readers— all two of them.

There was a pile of Eagle A typewriter boxes in an even stack under the worktable. I got them out and started to go through them. Most were Brady's own productions: Max Brady hard-boiled specials or rape-and-ravage Melissa Crowells with titles like *Raging Passions* and *Wild Savage Affair*. High-concept titles.

There was another stack of boxes behind the first. I got these out. The first three were Verna Trains, straight historical romances and contemporary "noncategories." A "noncategory" romance is a category romance over ninety thousand words. Looking over the first chapters, I thought Brady had little feeling for romance of the nonviolent variety. The books he wrote for Verna were full of fainting virgins and mysteriously powerful heroes— stock romance stereotyping circa 1954. No wonder Verna's books weren't making any money.

The last two boxes in the stack were the first two parts of a long and lugubriously written mainstream novel on the publishing business. Max had written a forward saying that he knew nothing like this ever got past the hatchet men of the publishing mafia, but he was determined to leave a record of the Truth. I cringed. God only knows how many people out there are determined to leave a record of the Truth, by which they usually mean their favorite conspiracy theory. Max's was a dilly. He thought Simon & Schuster was in league with the White House and Mobil Oil to suppress any portrayal of American Life as It Really Is.

American Life as It Really Is was presented most accurately in the novels of Max Brady.

Right.

I went out to the kitchen to look for rat poison. I found several thousand cockroaches and an unopened tin of boric acid. People use boric acid for cockroaches because it's reputed not to kill pets.

I went back to the worktable and sat in Max's chair. I was beginning to wonder what I had come looking for. Evidence that he'd ghosted both Verna's and Marilou's romantic suspense novels for Dana's line, certainly—but it wasn't here. Evidence that he had access to arsenic, rat poison, cockroach poison. That wasn't here either. I was beginning to feel a little silly. What would I have done with that stuff if I'd found it?

I started rocking back and forth in Max's chair. I wanted A Plan. I wanted to know What I Was Supposed to Do Next. It occurred to me that I approached murders the way I had once approached writing romance novels. I wanted to proceed with a rigid, predetermined outline, all possibilities covered, the threat of surprise neutralized. Murders never seemed to oblige.

I was still rocking in the chair when the good luck and bad luck hit me at once. The good luck was that I went rummaging through Max's typewriter ribbon box—more as a result of nervous energy than any directed search—and came up with Caroline Dooley's crystal monogrammed paperweight.

The bad luck was that I looked up at a sound from the hall and found Max coming through his front door.

It happened so fast, I just sat there, weighing the crystal paperweight in my hand and letting my mouth hang open. It struck me I'd been wrong about Max. With his denim jacket off and the sleeves of his shirt rolled up, he was thin but not puny. The muscles in his forearms were well developed. His shoulders strained the seams of his shirt. I sent up a prayer that he was dead drunk.

"Oh, fine," he said. "I've now become the target of Pay McKenna, Girl Sleuth."

I coughed and went for my cigarettes. "I came looking for you," I said. "The door—"

"The door was locked when I left," Max said. "I remember locking it. I'm not drunk all the time."

"Right," I said.

"Put the paperweight down," Max said. "I already told Caroline it was me. Not that she hadn't had it figured out anyway."

I put the paperweight on the worktable. Max threw himself on the bed, oblivious to the mess. We sat staring at each other for a while. I was at a complete loss for words. I still thought Max had killed Verna and Sarah, though I thought he'd meant to kill Marilou. He'd admitted to wrecking Caroline's office, hadn't he? I must have been wrong when I'd said the same person couldn't have wrecked that office and poisoned Sarah in the same lunch hour. Max must have found a way to do it. I brushed away the nervousness I felt at the sloppiness of the explanation. Details. I could get to the details later.

Max took out a pack of unfiltered Camels, lit one, and tossed the spent match into his sheets. He smelled like stale beer.

"Shit," he said. "The stupid thing about this is that I *want* to talk about this. I want to tell somebody. It's driving me crazy."

"What?"

"You had to break in on me?" Max said. "You couldn't call me up and use one of those clever little Agatha Christie ruses the papers are always talking about?"

"I was at the 42nd Street Library and I just came over," I said, thinking it was best to ignore the break-in as far as possible. "You want to tell me why you killed Verna and Sarah English?"

"Are you out of your *mind?*" Max's eyes were coming out of his head. "That's the kind of thing I mean," he said, calmer. "That's why I want to talk to somebody. Everybody's probably running around convinced I bumped off my primary meal ticket and some poor little slob from the provinces I didn't even know."

"I thought maybe you were gunning for Marilou," I said. "You wrote her book, didn't you? The one for Dana?"

"Yeah. Most of the books in the series. But for God's sake, if I wanted to bump off Marilou Saunders, I could have done a better job of it. You in the hospital. Some poor schmuck of a civilian dead. Where was the planning in that? Where was the common sense, for that matter?"

"Plans go wrong," I said.

He rubbed his lips. "Look," he said. "I'm a hack, right? Okay, I don't say so right out loud, and I don't say so even to myself most of the time, but that's what I am. I'm never going to be Raymond Chandler, or Dashiell Hammett, or even Erle Stanley Gardner. I'm just not good enough." He bit his lip. He smiled. "You heard it here first," he said. "But it's the truth. And another part of that truth is that I make my living, such as it is, ghostwriting, writing under pseudonyms, writing to order whenever I can get the work. Verna—" He got off the bed and started pacing, as far as that was possible, among the debris. "Caroline Dooley is a grade-A bitch," he said. "So I'm a hack. She uses hacks all the time. She didn't have to sabotage my book. It wasn't any of her goddamned business if I was helping Dana out. It wasn't any of her business and it wasn't any of her concern."

"You're not making any sense," I said.

"No?" Max said. "Try this. Somebody's trying to kill me."

"Of course," I said, thinking of the half-finished mainstream novel on the floor. Paranoia, paranoia. I wondered how drunk Max was. I wondered how drunk he had to be to admit he was a hack.

He stopped next to a cardboard chest of drawers and leaned against it. "I put it wrong," he said. "I should have said somebody ought to be trying to kill me. As far as I can figure out. Because—"

"Because?" I prompted him.

"It had to be Caroline Dooley," he said. "It had to be Caroline Dooley trying to sabotage Dana's line. That's the only thing I can think of. I figured whoever put the poison in Dana's office had to be after you."

"I didn't have anything to do with Dana's line," I said.

"You were bringing her writers," Max said.

"I brought her a writer she sold to Caroline," I said. "Why

would Caroline try to kill me for bringing a writer to Dana that Dana then sold to her?"

Max sat back down on the bed. "I don't know," he said. "I don't know."

He put his head in his hands and his elbows on his knees and rocked. I watched him, wondering what it was all supposed to mean. The sick feeling in the middle of my stomach was the knowledge that my theory was disintegrating. I could no longer honestly believe Max Brady had killed one, possibly two, people. The police say there is no such thing as a "murderer type," but Max *wasn't the type.* He wasn't guilty. He wasn't afraid-of-being-caught. He was just afraid.

"Why?" I asked him. "Why did you rip up Caroline's office?"

"I was drunk," he shrugged. "I was furious. I'd found out about the sabotage—God, all this stuff about things getting deliberately misshipped, I don't know. It was baroque. And I was furious and drunk and—"

"But who told you about it?" I said. "Where did you hear about it?"

"I don't know. I was drinking with some people. Dana. DeAndrea. What's her name, Verna's friend with the beads all over her dresses—"

"Amelia Samson."

"Yeah, right. Anyway, lots of people. Marilou Saunders came by." He grinned. "She wanted to see Dana but not me. I'm not supposed to exist. Nothing's supposed to remind her she didn't write that dreck herself."

"Does Dana know?"

"Hell, yes. She got me into this. You're not supposed to know. This is a deep, dark secret. For real, for once. If that old bitch Dooley knew, she wouldn't have to kill people. Or so I'm told."

"Does Dana know you wrote Verna's book?"

"I didn't write Verna's book," Max said. "Not this one. She didn't need me."

"Are you sure?"

"I wrote Verna's last five books before this one. Of course I'm sure. We had a thing going a while back and it was over, but I still liked the old bat. And the money was good. And the aggravations minimal."

"Verna wrote her own book?"

"Far as I know. She didn't say anything about getting another ghost. And she would have. We still talked. She didn't like having to use a ghost."

I shook my head. "It doesn't make sense," I said. "The wrong people are dead to make killing them to protect Dana's line make any sense. Even if you assume the target in the reception room was Marilou Saunders. Something tells me Marilou's ego is big enough, she'd sue man or beast who said she hadn't written her book herself. If Marilou did it, she had to be trying to kill Sarah specifically, and that doesn't make sense either."

"Caroline Dooley," Max said. "I told you."

I brushed it away. "Somebody told you there'd been sabotage on your book. *My Rod Is Hot*? That book?"

Max nodded. "Hope springs eternal," he said.

"What did you do then?"

"Drank," he said. "Drank some more. Got pissed off as well as pissed. DeAndrea and Dana took me home. I passed out. I got up and drank some more. I got furious again. And—well—" He smiled sheepishly. "I guess I was playing detective. Anyway, I thought if I searched her office I could find the evidence, that she'd screwed me, so I went over there and waited until lunchtime—"

"Hiding a razor in your coat?"

"I'd just bought some new blades. I don't know. Anyway, I got in there and there wasn't any evidence, but there was all this romantic suspense. The place was lousy with romantic suspense."

"So you ripped it up."

"I guess so. But McKenna, I never went near Dana's office. That day or any other day. I've never been in the place. With my ex-wife's penchant for hiring detectives, I don't dare. So I didn't poison anyone."

"You could have taken care of Caroline's office while someone else took care of the poisoning," I said. "An accomplice."

"Who?" Max said. "And for what?"

"I don't know. But Caroline's keys were stolen. If you didn't take them, who did? And if you took them, where are they? Did you give them to someone?"

"As far as I know, I never had Caroline Dooley's keys. The paperweight, yes. It made me sick listening to her go on and on about that paperweight. But as far as I know, I never had the keys."

"As far as you know?"

"After I left her office, I went out and had a few more drinks."

"Right," I said.

"You go ask DeAndrea," Max said. "He was with me the whole time afterward. I think maybe it was, like, more than one day. Days."

I sighed. It could have been days, the way Max had been drinking lately.

"And he'll tell you," Max said, "that I don't have anything to do with poisons. I don't keep them in the apartment. I won't even kill roaches with them. Just ask him."

"All right," I said. "I'll ask him." This time I was the one biting my lip, rubbing my face, going through the stock sequence of nervous gestures. Poison, poison, poison. Every time somebody said the word "poison"—not arsenic, but *"poison"*—something went off in my head. Something felt wrong, strangely out of place. Every time it happened, I tried to figure out what it was, and couldn't.

Maybe I *would* talk to DeAndrea.

TWENTY-THREE

As soon as I hit the street, I knew I wasn't going to go looking for DeAndrea immediately. I was exhausted, and confused, and *rebellious.* I hated the idea that Max's assault on Caroline's office had been a fluke, a side issue, with no connection to Verna, or Sarah, or the precise placement of arsenic in Dana Morton's reception room. Max's neighborhood didn't make me feel much better. I made a few halfhearted phone calls from the one working booth at the corner of Eleventh and Thirty-ninth, got no answer at either DeAndrea's apartment or Bogie's, and gave up without a qualm. I bought cigarettes in a bodega that should have had a sign in the window saying "No English Spoken Here." I went hunting for cabs. I had to walk all the way to Eighth Avenue before I found one.

Phoebe had not only taken Adrienne to Eeyore's, she'd hit the children's department at Saks, F.A.O. Schwarz, Baskin-Robbins, Laura Ashley, children's furniture at Bloomingdale's, and Crazy Eddie. My apartment looked like page 3 of *New York* magazine's "Best Bets for Christmas." My hallway looked like the back end of a grocery store half an hour after a major delivery. My kitchen looked like the art department at Fires of Love, with one exception. The three oversized easels with romantic suspense cover paintings on them—man and girl fleeing gunmen, girl in off-the-shoulder peasant blouse and four-inch heels; man and girl scaling Alp, girl in off-the-shoulder peasant blouse and four-inch heels; man and girl hiding in bowels of boat, girl in off-the-shoulder peasant blouse and four-inch heels—looked right in place, but the pyramid of marzipan frogs in the center of the table looked a little odd. Phoebe had cleaned out my ashtray to put the frogs in, so I made a makeshift one out of AWR letterhead and lit a cigarette.

Phoebe came out of the back hall and said, "I ordered you a couch."

"Why not?" I said. "You ordered everything else. What is all this stuff?"

"Furniture for Adrienne's room." She sat down in the chair opposite me. "I unpacked it and left it in the living room because I'm too small to move it. Nick's coming over later."

I took a very long drag. "Peachy keen," I said.

"Adrienne and I saw you on television," she said.

"Let's not talk about it," I said. "Let's especially not talk about it around Nick. He saw it, too."

"It made the wire services," Phoebe said. "They've heard about it in *Russia.*"

I made an appropriate groan and decided to chain-smoke. There didn't seem to be anything else to do. My life was a mess, the case (if that's what you wanted to call it) was a worse mess, Nick was going to stop speaking to me when he found out what I'd been up to all afternoon, Dana had probably already stopped speaking to me, if she wasn't pretending never to have heard of me, Marilou would undoubtedly sue me . . .

"Sometimes," I told Phoebe, "I think Myrra is watching over me, making sure my life is always interesting."

"I know," Phoebe said. "Before Myrra, your life was normal."

"Normal for Manhattan, anyway."

"I've got bad news," Phoebe said. "Adrienne may be only seven, but she reads newspapers. She got it from the *Times.*"

I looked across the living room in the direction of the back hall, feeling guilty at feeling so relieved. Whatever happened now, I wouldn't have to break the news. I wouldn't have to watch Adrienne's face come apart under the impact. The worst had already happened. I could go in there and do what I felt capable of doing—holding the pieces together.

"Pay?" Phoebe said. "Nick said something about—are you going to keep her? Adopt her, I mean?"

"I don't know," I said. "I haven't really thought about it. When we were in Holbrook, I just wanted—"

"To get her away from Cassie Arbeth," Phoebe said. "I know, I know. I don't blame you. But Pay, I think we should talk about it."

"About what? Keeping Adrienne?"

"I think maybe if you don't want to do it, I do. I mean, David and I are fighting right now, but we wouldn't be if I'd marry him and then all we'd have to worry about is our being Jewish and Adrienne not, that might worry social services, but—"

I gave her a long look. "Does Adrienne want to stay?" I asked her.

"I think so."

"Does she know who she wants to stay with—you or me?"

"Well, actually, I don't think she thinks it makes a difference."

"It probably doesn't," I said. "Around here, it's mostly all or nothing." I shoved my cigarettes into my pocket and got up. "How's she doing? Why did you leave her alone?"

"She wanted to be alone," Phoebe said. "I think she wants to talk to you. As to how she is—" Phoebe shrugged. "She's a funny kid, Patience."

"No funnier than I am."

Phoebe made a face. "Don't tell me. She reminds you of you when you were a child."

"No," I said. "You remind me of me when I was a child. Adrienne reminds me of me *now.*"

I headed into the back hall.

It wasn't hard to find the room she'd picked, even in the endless corridor that was the "bedroom wing." Most of the doors in the "bedroom wing" were open, revealing empty rooms and ancient carpeting. The corner room on the right was shut up tight. I stopped outside and knocked. Nothing at all came from within, not even breathing. I knocked again.

There was, quite literally, the patter of little feet. The door creaked open. A face popped out and stared at my knees.

"You're home," Adrienne said.

"Can I come in and talk?"

"Phoebe bought me a television set."

She turned around and padded back into the room, opening the door as she went. Most of her new furniture was still in my living room, but Phoebe had managed to drag the television in. It stood against the north wall, thirty-six-inch screen staring blankly at the mullioned windows overlooking Central Park, fifty-six knobs polished and winking even in the half-gray late-fall afternoon light, computer clock winking, light meters and sound meters and recording monitors still but ready, double VCR hook-ups closed against the possibility of dust.

"Dear God," I said. "You could drive that thing to Connecticut."

"It's got a computer in it," Adrienne said. "I don't know how it works yet."

"I wouldn't know how to turn the damn thing *on.*"

Adrienne nodded wisely. "You have to be *very careful* when you tell Phoebe you want something."

She sat cross-legged on the floor and put her hands in Camille's fur. Since Adrienne arrived, Camille had shown no interest in me whatsoever. She sprawled in Adrienne's lap, belly up to encourage scratching in all the right places. I sat on the floor, dancer's one fluid motion. Adrienne nodded, solemn.

"I saw them do that at school once," she said. "In a school film. Ballet dancers."

"It's not hard," I said. "I could teach you to do that."

"Phoebe says you don't like televisions. That's why we put it in here."

I hadn't had a television since finding Julie Simms's body in my Eighty-second Street apartment, that was true, but I didn't think it had anything to do with how I felt about televisions. I had taken nothing, not even clothes, from that apartment. I kept imagining I could smell death on them.

"Mama used to say watching too much television rots your brain," Adrienne said. "She said that was what was wrong with Mrs. Arbeth and the other people on the street. They watched so much television they couldn't think anymore, and then they just sat around and didn't do anything."

"Ah," I said.

"I don't really think it was that," Adrienne said. She seemed to be working something immensely difficult through her head. "It's like being good and bad in church," she said. "Like they tell you in church. I don't know how to say it."

I stretched out on my stomach, elbows on the floor, chin in hands, so I was close enough to touch her if she looked like she wanted to be touched. Her face was still screwed into the pain of effort. Her hands were balled into fists.

"Moral and immoral," I said. "Those are the words. Moral means what you're supposed to do, and immoral means doing what's bad. You think what Mrs. Arbeth does is something bad like stealing or telling a lie—"

Adrienne's face cleared. "Yeah," she said. "Only I can't get it exactly. I mean, Mrs. Arbeth doesn't *do* anything. Only the not doing anything is as bad as stealing or telling a lie, only I don't know why."

"There are a lot of really brilliant people out there who spent a whole lot of time trying to figure that one out," I said. "Did you used to go to church?"

"Sometimes. Sometimes Mama writes Sundays. She goes to work the rest of the week." She scowled. "Mrs. Arbeth doesn't even go to *work,*" she said. "And she never cleans the house."

I tugged at her hair. "You want to talk about your mother?"

Adrienne drew her knees close to her chest, squishing the cat. The cat didn't mind. I lay on my stomach, wondering what that kid's IQ was.

"Is my mama going to be a book?" Adrienne asked.

"That she is."

"A real book or a paper book?"

Fine, I thought. A future editor of the *Times Book Review.* "A real book," I said. "Maybe a paper book later. Lots of times you're a real book first—"

Adrienne shook this away. "As long as she's a real book. That's what she wanted. She wanted to be a real book and then

she wanted us to move away from Holbrook and come to live in
New York. Am I going to do what Phoebe says? Live in New
York with you and her?"

"Do you want to? Don't you have grandparents, or—"

"Oh, we didn't have those. Mama told me. Her mama died
and she was the only one left."

That might or might not be true, but I didn't want to upset
Adrienne, so I said nothing. Adrienne had tightened her hold on
her knees.

"If Mama's going to be a book and I'm going to live in New
York, it's all *right,*" she said, frantic. "I mean, not all right, but
it's the important thing. She said—" Adrienne stopped. There
were tears. She didn't want tears. I wanted to tell her it was all
right. She was supposed to cry. No seven-year-old had to be in
complete control of her emotions. I couldn't think of what to say
or how to say it. I knew how she felt. I hadn't cried in front of
another human being since I was her age. A combination of pride
and stubbornness and the fear of vulnerability makes me never
want to do it again. I wanted to tell her to let go, but even
thinking the words made me feel like a phony. I wouldn't want to
let go. I want to win a victory over tears.

"She wanted something and she went out and got it," Adrienne said tremulously. "She told me about that. That's the most
important thing. She told me over and over. She wanted something and she didn't sit around wishing for it or saying there was
nothing she could do about anything, she went out and got it.
And if she got it, then it's all right because she said that was the
point, the point of—"

I got her a second before she fell. I caught her coming forward,
wrapped my arms around her, held her close. There was no answer to this, no explanation, nothing that could ever make it
right. That was the truth. That was a truth hard to tell an adult,
never mind a seven-year-old child.

"What I want," Adrienne said, "is to bring her *back.*"

"I know," I said. "I know. I want to bring her back, too."

"No one can bring her back," Adrienne said. "I've been thinking about it and thinking about it. Nobody can bring her back. And I get so *angry.*"

"Everybody gets angry," I said. "Everybody thinks crazy things like maybe it was their fault." She jerked in my arms. I was right on target. "None of that matters," I said. "None of it's true. You're going to feel bad for a while. That's all right. You have a right to feel bad and you *have* to feel bad before you can feel good again. Only it helps to feel bad with company. Even if you don't like to cry."

She wriggled out of my arms and wiped her eyes with the back of her hand. "It *wasn't* my fault," she said. "Somebody did it on purpose."

"Yes, they did."

"Is that the same thing? As Mrs. Arbeth? Is making someone dead—"

"Murdering someone."

"Is that like Mrs. Arbeth?"

"That's worse than Mrs. Arbeth. Mrs. Arbeth can always get religion someday and straighten herself out."

Adrienne treated me to a good, healthy grimace of contempt. I couldn't help a smile. We both knew Cassie Arbeth was going to straighten herself out around the time the United States and Russia implemented a viable nuclear arms reduction pact.

Adrienne yawned. "I want to go to sleep," she said. "But I think Phoebe wants me to watch 'Sesame Street.' "

"You can't watch 'Sesame Street' until we get the cable hooked up. There's no reception in this part of Manhattan. I'll put you to bed in my room."

"Don't forget the cat," Adrienne said.

I couldn't have forgotten the cat if I'd wanted to. Camille had attached herself to Adrienne's brand-new Saks Fifth Avenue cardigan.

By the time I put them down in my bed, they were both already asleep.

In the kitchen, Phoebe was icing butter cookies to look like jack-o'-lanterns. The butter cookies were spread across the AWR stationery and the romantic suspense posters, letting them know what was what. I made a stack of iced butter cookies and started eating them.

"Had lunch with Amelia," I said. "Never got a chance to eat anything."

"You going to tell me what was wrong with Verna and Amelia?"

"Later. And I'll have to swear you to secrecy."

"So swear me. How was Adrienne?"

"Okay, I think. Rocky but okay. She went to sleep in my room." I tried a marzipan frog. My stomach decided it didn't like me anymore.

Televisions, I thought. Televisions, televisions. What was wrong with televisions? I took a piece of AWR letterhead, turned it upside down so that I had a blank sheet, and began to make doodles in the upper right-hand corner with a green razor point. Televisions.

"Phoebe," I said. "Did you say something last night about televisions? About Adrienne never had a television?"

"That's right," Phoebe swatted my hand away from a new stack of butter cookies. "She had to go over to that awful woman's house to watch television."

"You remember when we went into Sarah's half of the house? When Adrienne was packing and we were cleaning up after the robbery?"

"You were cleaning up after the robbery."

"Phoebe," I said. "If there wasn't a television, what did they steal?"

Phoebe stopped icing her cookies. She frowned. "Maybe they didn't steal anything. They came in and there was nothing to steal, so they left."

"They took out a couple of drawers in the meantime."

"Pique."

"If it was pique, they'd have trashed the place," I said. "That sort usually do. Also, think about what got handled. Sarah's desk. The writing desk in Sarah's room. The drawers in the vanity table. Nothing else."

"So?"

I wrote "Revised Schedule" on top of the sheet in front of me, then:

Thurs./Fri.: Verna dies.
Fri. lunch: Sarah, me poisoned at Dana's.
            Caroline's office vandalized.
Weekend: Sarah's house robbed.
Mon.: Sarah's body found in Caroline's apartment. Fire.

I pushed the paper across the table.

"I left out the important thing about the fire," I said. "Somebody burned a lot of papers and a manuscript. That was it."

"So?"

"I tried to make a list like this at Nick's this morning," I said, "but I got sidetracked. I'd have left out the robbery then anyway. But look at this. Somebody robs Sarah's house and disturbs a lot of papers but doesn't take anything that we can figure out. Somebody goes to Caroline's apartment, puts Sarah's body in a chair, then rips up a manuscript and burns every paper in the place. Max said he vandalized Caroline's office all on his own, but he could have been put up to it, couldn't he?"

"Max Brady ripped up Caroline Dooley's *office?*" Phoebe said.

"We've all been assuming Sarah wasn't really a target," I said, "because there didn't seem to be any point. Marilou, yes. Me, it's happened before. But what if killing Sarah was the whole point?"

"What for?"

"She sent that manuscript to the whole world," I said. "She sent it to Verna. According to Amelia, Verna was burned out. She couldn't write to save her life. According to Max, he didn't write Verna's romantic suspense."

"You think Verna took Sarah's manuscript and handed it in as her own?"

"Maybe."

"But Verna died before Sarah did."

"Verna wasn't the only one with a stake in Verna Train novels." I reached for the phone. "As far as I can tell, she wasn't even the one with the biggest stake in Verna Train novels."

I dialed Max Brady's apartment, let the phone ring two dozen times (twelve rings to the minute, according to the phone company), hung up, and tried DeAndrea's place. No answer there either. I got up and headed into the hall for my coat.

"It all comes down to Max," I said. "No matter how I look at it, it always comes down to Max."

"You think Max killed Sarah?"

"No," I said. "I think if I can keep Max sober long enough, he can tell me who killed Sarah. Even if he doesn't think he knows."

"Oh, fine," Phoebe said. "Where are you going?"

I was halfway through the hall. "Bogie's," I called back. "If DeAndrea isn't there, Karen and Billy may know where Max is."

TWENTY-FOUR

Billy and Karen may have known where Max Brady was, but I didn't get a chance to ask them. By the time I got to Bogie's, Billy was pinned behind the bar by a group of jump-the-gun Happy Hour freaks and Karen was on the sidewalk, surrounded by a circle of women who wanted more than anything to know how to deck a man three times their size with a flick of the wrist. Actually, it was more like a flick of the foot. As I came out of the cab, she had her foot hooked around the poor man's leg and was tripping him forward. He fell sideways. Hopping.

DeAndrea was sitting on a barstool in a corner near the window, squinting over a stack of papers. He cleared a space for me.

"Ah," he said. "You've come to the meeting."

"Meeting?"

"Never mind." He did his best to signal Billy for me, got a kind of baleful glare, and shrugged. "There's an MWA dinner meeting tonight," he said. "Here."

"Oh," I said.

"Don't worry about it," he said. "As far as I can tell, with the possible exception of Mary Higgins Clark, people attend MWA meetings in inverse proportion to the money they're making."

I got out my cigarettes and lit one. "I came down to find Max Brady," I said.

"Go ahead and find him," DeAndrea said. "Last time I saw him, he was passed out on the bed in my apartment. He rouses periodically to use the facilities."

"He's drunk."

"As a skunk."

Billy came rushing down to our end of the bar, took my order for a Bloody Mary, and went rushing back. The Happy Hour group was ordering pousse-cafés. Out on the sidewalk, Karen's anonymous volunteer was windmilling, trying to prevent himself from falling backward. Billy came back with the Bloody Mary.

"It's this business with Caroline Dooley sabotaging his book," I said. "And then the keys. He says he never had the keys—"

"Keys?" DeAndrea said. "Yeah, he had Caroline Dooley's keys. After he ripped up Austin, Stoddard & Trapp. Dana and I found him at O'Lunney's with all this *stuff* on him. That paperweight thing. Keys. People's manuscripts."

"People's manuscripts?"

"Yeah. He must have gone out of there looking like Santa Claus, no joke. Security at that place must be dreadful."

"What happened to the keys?"

"I put them in an envelope and addressed them to AST and Dana went off and mailed them. We didn't think we could trust Max with the keys. I was a *little* pissed off, if you want to know the truth. I mean, she got him started on that nonsense to begin with. Caroline's doing this to your book. Caroline's doing that to your book. Caroline wasn't doing anything to his book. It was an awful book."

"Dana," I said. I put my hand in my pocket, looking for a fresh pack of cigarettes, and hit metal. I pulled the little silver thing into the light and stared at it, resentful.

"Look at this." I held it out to DeAndrea. "What is it?"

He took it out of my hand. "A little silver thing," he said.

I put it on the bar next to my drink. Outside, the male volunteer was going to his knees.

"Television sets," I said. "And poison. And *this* thing."

"What?"

"I don't know what. It's got something to do with Sarah's manuscript. Only I don't know what. And the thing about the poison—" I shrugged. "It's like there are little pieces of things floating around in my head. Something I know about the poison that I can't remember. Something wrong. And Dana. You said Dana and something hit me. Like, if I could shift gears somewhere, I'd know something about Dana. Only I don't know what."

"At least you've given up on Max," DeAndrea said. "That was a dead end. Believe me. He might be capable sober, but the way things have been—"

Bill responded to a signal for another Bloody Mary by raising his eyes to the ceiling and pretending to search there for vodka. Outside, Karen started to approach her volunteer from behind, inching closer, gesturing with her hands.

"Max could have been in it with someone," I said.

"Sure," DeAndrea said. "He'd be the perfect accomplice. He couldn't turn you in because he couldn't remember doing anything."

Billy put another Bloody Mary, this time with celery, in front of me. I took the celery out. On the sidewalk, Karen's victim fell backward, pitched forward, was caught by the crowd.

It almost didn't register. I was looking at my list again, trying to work a rebus without clues, when it sank in.

"Jesus Christ," I said. "What did she do?" I got off my seat and headed for the sidewalk, running into a Yuppie couple on their way in.

DeAndrea got off his seat and ran after me. "It's all right," he yelled. "It's only a demonstration."

I wedged through the crowd, grabbed Karen, and spun her around.

"What did you do?" I asked her. "Just now. He fell backward and pitched forward. And then he sort of fell."

"It's all right," Karen said, looking a little panicked. "I was just—"

"What did you *do?*"

Karen spun at the male volunteer, hooked her ankle around his, and jerked. He fell backward. Then he pitched forward. Then he was in the air and floating toward the crowd.

Somebody caught him. I don't know who.

"Dear God," I said. "Phoebe was right."

"Rape strategy," Karen said. "It's not really martial arts, it's just this thing you learn to ward off rape—"

"Rape," I said.

Karen didn't like my tone. "I'm not in favor of it," she said.

"Rape," I said again.

I had grabbed the little silver thing when I ran from the bar. I was holding it in the palm of my hand, squeezing it, almost cutting myself. Now I held it out and stared at it.

"Jesus Christ," I said.

"What's the little silver thing," Karen said.

I put it in my pocket. "It's a pen clip," I said. "It's the silver T-clip from a Tiffany T-pen."

"McKenna?" Karen said. "Are you all right?"

I got a ten-dollar bill from my back pocket and thrust it into her hand. "To pay Billy for the drinks," I said. "I've got to find a cab."

TWENTY-FIVE

At the last minute, I called Phoebe and left a message for Nick. I could have called Nick—it was only five-thirty and he was likely to be at the office—but I didn't want a lecture and I didn't want a shouting match. I got out of the cab a block above Dana's building, tried three ruined pay phones before I was able to get a half-decent connection on a fourth, and told Phoebe,

"I'll be home in less than an hour. Tell him I've got to see Tony Marsh official-unofficial. He knows how to set that up."

"Where are you?"

"Trying to catch Dana before she leaves the office."

"McKenna—"

I hung up. If Phoebe spent any time thinking about it, she'd realize *no one* went looking for Dana at five-thirty. Dana liked to do things during business hours. Dana broke routine only for large deals involving multimillion-dollar offers from German paperback houses. I was hoping it had been a dead week. I didn't want to find Dana or talk to her. I wanted to search her files.

Somewhere in those files was a copy of Verna Train's romantic suspense novel. Sarah's novel wouldn't be there, but I had a copy of that at home. I had to have the two manuscripts together to be absolutely sure.

I got off the elevator at twenty-six to find a dead floor. The lights were off in the reception room. The typewriter was put away. The green Dripmaster had been washed, dried, and turned on its head. I sat down. The manuscript was the most important thing, but not the only thing. Now that I was in Dana's office, I could think of a few items it wouldn't hurt to clean up before I got home to Nick's apoplexy and Tony's inevitable skepticism.

Like where Sarah's body had been when the police searched the office.

Like how Sarah and I had both managed to take arsenic when it had only been intended for one of us.

Like, where the arsenic had come from.

I got out of my chair and headed for the center offices, trying to think of a reasonable explanation for being there if someone happened to be wandering around. First the general file room, then Dana's office. I could always say I had come to look for Dana. No one would believe it, but I could say it.

I was out of the office and down the hall before it hit me. I had to back all the way up to be sure I wasn't imagining things.

The green plastic Dripmaster.

The day Sarah died, it had been a blue plastic Dripmaster.

I walked across the carpet and touched it. On the floor in the corner I could see a small plastic dish of rat pellets. I had a sudden vision of myself spilling coffee into that corner while Sarah lurched around the reception room. There had been no plastic dish of rat pellets there then. There *had* been such a dish when I first came in to see Dana. A full dish.

All she'd had to do was dump the dish into the Dripmaster. She could have done it with Sarah in the room. She could have shielded the Dripmaster with her body while she "made coffee," electric coffeemaker blend plus rat pellets. The water would have dissolved enough of them as it went through.

When she found me lying on the floor with the line open to 911, all she had to do was chuck the Dripmaster, hollow out one or two Halloween candies and put pellets in them, hide Sarah's body, and wait. Of course, she hadn't realized there would be Marilou to contend with. As it turned out, it didn't matter. Marilou didn't want to talk any more than Dana wanted her to.

Where had she hidden Sarah's body? Where, for that matter, had she hidden the Dripmaster and the plastic dish for the rat pellets?

I started back toward the central offices.

———

The halls were dead dark and I was a little punchy. I wandered in and out of offices, around and around corridors, up and down back hallways. In the dark, Dana's offices seemed endless, convoluted, sinister. In a suite full of paper, there are paper rustles, paper sighs, paper complaints. Paper shudders and snaps in the ghost breezes, the ghost drafts. Writers' offices, literary agents' offices, publishing houses all sound like haunted mansions after dark.

I held my breath, tried a door, looked in, found a ladies' room. I tried another door and found a storage closet full of oversized black plastic garbage bags. The garbage bags made me hesitate, but I couldn't decide what they made me think of. I closed the door and moved on. I could always come back, I told myself. My subconscious added, "in the morning." The last thing I wanted was to go wandering around those offices any longer than I had to.

I no longer wanted to go wandering around those offices at all. I have, at various times in my life, broken into offices, apartments, and hotel suites after hours. I am always very brave going in and very chicken when I get there. I was very chicken now. Dana's offices were spooking the hell out of me. I was beginning to think I'd arrived on the tail wind of a brainstorm. I should have tried to get Tony to listen to me first. Then if I met too much resistance, I could have tried to find out for myself. I could—

I had been moving while I was thinking. In the dark I hadn't noticed the door. Even if I had, I'd have had no reason to expect it to be open. It was a big, ugly, splintered-wood double door, the kind often locked and barred to make a wall in a makeshift room. There had been "walls" like that at Farret and Writing Enterprises. I was so used to ancient-door-used-as-wall, I would never have tried to open it. I didn't have to. I leaned against it. It pitched me into the hall.

It pitched me into more than the hall. It sent me sprawling headfirst across a utility corridor into a set of freight elevator doors. Those, too, were ancient and wooden. They swung on hinges instead of sliding on tracks. They opened whether the carriage was on that floor or not.

I caught myself right before I fell into the tangle of wires on top of the elevator cage. Caught myself and stopped, looking down at the gears and cables and electric lines.

Looking down at the body of Radd Stassen, his ankle caught in a rope, his mouth stretched into a maniac's grin.

I was wondering what had made him die grinning when I heard her voice at the end of the hall.

"Some people," she said, "are hell-bent on suicide."

It was a duet for stringed instruments: Dana at one end, me in front of the swinging doors of that freight elevator, fuses blown and windows blocked by black construction paper. We were two ghosts talking in the dark.

I couldn't see if she was holding a weapon. I couldn't see her face.

"That's where Sarah's body was," I said. "On top of the elevator cage. When the police wanted the elevator, they rang for it. It wouldn't have occurred to them to open the doors before the cage got here. Or you ran down and sent the elevator up a few floors. Either way."

"Why in the name of God would I want to kill a first novelist —a first *romantic suspense* novelist, for God's sake?"

"For the same reason you had to kill him," I gestured at Radd Stassen. "The Gallard Rowson line's a sham, Dana. Ghostwritten from start to finish, contract or no contract. Max Brady did most of it. I sent you Sarah's manuscript and you stole it whole. Mostly the slush pile isn't worth bothering with, but Sarah was an exception. I kept thinking it was Verna who must have stolen it, and as long as I did, things wouldn't come together. Verna was supposed to have stolen Amelia's outline, but I'm beginning not to think so. No matter what she told Amelia. I think you stole that, too."

"Ask Amelia's little secretary. She says it was Verna."

"You could have paid her for that." I started inching away from the elevator shaft. Even if Dana didn't have a weapon, she could rush me. If she rushed me, I might lose my balance and fall. I didn't want to end up on the top of that elevator cage with Radd Stassen's body.

Unfortunately, Dana was between me and the exit. The only way I could move was back toward the windows, into a corner.

"Gallard Rowson wouldn't take ghostwritten," I said. "That was in the contract. They would have ruined you if they'd found out what you were doing."

"Gallard Rowson takes what I give them. I don't tell anybody anything they don't want to hear."

"You used to have a lot of hot-shit writers, but you don't anymore," I said. "You got into genre much too late, so you had to go all out. You had no track record in packaging. You had to give Gallard Rowson something. They wanted brand names and celebrities really writing their own books. They wanted personal revelations they could sell to the readers."

"It's been very successful. The initial subscription is through the ceiling."

"It won't stay that way if the books are awful. There isn't any way you could give Gallard Rowson what they were asking for. Marilou Saunders can't write, and neither can the rest of your celebrities. And your romance writers aren't romantic suspense writers. You had to have the books and the plots and the characters, not just the bylines. And you had only one way to get them. Ghosts. Max. Cheating."

"So what?"

"If it came out, Gallard Rowson would dump you."

"Maybe. And maybe not."

"You couldn't take the chance, Dana. You're the packager. Gallard Rowson pays the advances, but the authors contract with you. They work for you. A few of those people probably wanted, and got, guarantees. Like Marilou Saunders. Whether the book is published or not, they get paid. Whether it makes royalties or not, they get paid. And you pay them."

"This is getting positively baroque," Dana said.

I took a deep breath. Was I imagining it, or was Radd Stassen beginning to smell? I was probably imagining it, but imagining it was enough.

"It wouldn't have mattered if Jane Herman hadn't sold Sarah's novel to Caroline. If Sarah had sold it somewhere else, you could have blamed Verna for stealing it, but with it coming out of your own agency, you were going to get looked at more closely than you could allow. And you couldn't afford that. You had to make the whole situation go away. And you almost did."

"No 'almost' about it, Patience. Truly."

"Radd Stassen was checking into Max Brady, so you had to get rid of him. Maybe he found something. You put Sarah's body in a big plastic garbage bag and hid it here somewhere and then you had to stash it and you knew she'd be found, so you—what? Put it in a suitcase? You took it up the freight elevator in her building, that you must have done. And you set fire to the paper in there because you needed to call attention to Caroline. To anyone but yourself."

"Does this get better as it goes along?"

"You were looking for copies of Sarah's manuscript. You went out to Holbrook and searched her house. You got Max all worked up and made sure he'd do your dirty work at Caroline's office—"

"No," Dana said. "That I didn't do. I got him worked up, yes, but Caroline's office was a bonus. I hadn't expected that. It did save me some work."

"And it got you the keys."

"Oh yes. But I'd have got the keys anyway, Patience. One way or the other."

"You killed Verna because she was going to blow it. She realized it was Sarah's manuscript you were putting out as hers. What did you do—tell her it was a ghost deal? And when she found out it wasn't, she was going to talk? You killed Sarah because she would have talked, and she'd have insisted on her book being published as her book. You killed Radd Stassen because he was getting too close."

"But nobody killed Verna," Dana said gently. "Nobody could have. The police have gone on record with that."

"I was watching a demonstration today," I told her. "Self-defense techniques for rape attempts. I know how it was done, Dana. I know how the arsenic got into the coffee and how it got into the Halloween candy. I know everything but what happened to poor Radd Stassen. You'll probably tell me."

"No," Dana said.

I took the "little silver thing" out of my pocket. "This is yours," I said. "I must have taken it off you that day in the reception room. It's been bothering me ever since. You must have been moving Sarah's body and I must have seen. They said I wouldn't let go of it in the emergency room."

The silence was thick, heavy, motionless. I could feel her at the other end of the hall, shifting from foot to foot, getting ready to move toward me. I started to panic. Worse, I started to imagine things. I thought I heard the sound of the safety being clicked off on a gun. I thought I heard the sound of a knife being un-sheathed. I thought a lot of things that couldn't be true, because none of them were Dana's style. Dana would push. Dana would poison. Dana would never handle a weapon. It would be much too obvious.

Besides, I was looking right at her. Her hands were free.

I got my hands on the windowsill and pulled myself up until I was sitting on it, my legs swinging in the air. If she came too close, I could always kick. In the darkness, I might get away with it. I tried to keep my arms and torso tense, my legs loose and limber. I tried to remember what friends had told me about self-defense. It didn't help.

Dana was coming toward me, slowly, shuffling down the hall.

"I didn't know we'd sold that damn manuscript until you brought that little hick up here," she said. "I thought I had the thing taped. Jane must have said something, but I didn't realize it was the same one. If you hadn't brought Sarah up here, there really would have been a mess."

"This isn't a mess?"

"This is messy," Dana said. "There's a difference."

She fumbled with something, made a sound like breaking plastic, sighed. A flashlight went on in my face.

"If you don't get off that window," she said, "I'm going to break your ankle."

"I'll kick you," I said.

"Don't be childish," she said.

"Stop," Phoebe said. "Or I'll shoot."

It was so absurd, we were both caught in a kind of suspended animation. The idea of Phoebe (Weiss) Damereaux, four feet eleven, 130 pounds, everything-would-be-all-right-if-you'd-only-eat-more, pointing a gun at someone and spouting trite dialogue from a horse opera was enough to give anyone pause.

It gave Dana the idea she should turn around. She did, moving very slowly, pivoting on one heel, frowning.

As soon as she had her back to me, I jumped her.

I had her on the floor before I realized she had nothing but the flashlight in her hands after all.

EPILOGUE

We put Sarah down in what might very well have been the last private cemetery plot in Manhattan. I had to bribe my Aunt Eugenie (who owned the plot), and we had to agree to cremation and a silver urn in a marble box (to save space; Eugenie had every intention of being buried there, too), but we did it. Adrienne insisted on it. In the week since Dana Morton had been arrested, Adrienne had organized her grief. There were rituals to be performed, courtesies to be observed, poetic balances to be maintained. We brought Sarah's body to St. Thomas's churchyard in a stretch limousine. Everybody wore black.

Adrienne wore black wool from Lord & Taylor—$230 for a dress she would wear only once and would grow out of in a year. Phoebe had elected herself Arbiter of What Is Necessary for Children. I wanted to tell her I doubted if a shoemaker's daughter from Union City, New Jersey, spent her childhood in Lord & Taylor black, but I didn't. Her orientation made a peculiar kind of sense. Sarah had worked to make a certain kind of life for herself and Adrienne. Phoebe just wanted to make the dream come true.

Nick divorced himself from the funeral arrangements and went to work on Sarah's money. There was going to be a lot more of it than we thought at first. *Shadows in the Light* was not her only romantic suspense novel. There were six more. Like a lot of unpublished writers, Sarah had (sensibly) kept them in the mail. They started to drift back after stories about her appeared in the newspapers. They came with notes attached, "under the circumstances" notes. "Under the circumstances" in this case meant that everyone wanted to publish them, but they were Nice People and knew AST should have first crack. I found an agent happy to set up a bidding war, and Nick kept watch with a calculator.

The last I heard of Dana, she was accusing me of the murder of Verna Train. Dana had been getting fairly crazy since her arrest, and I had a feeling she was going to get crazier still. You cannot claim Extreme Emotional Disturbance unless you show signs of being Extremely Emotionally Disturbed.

"It was a mistake," I told Phoebe, on a late Monday afternoon about a week after the funeral. We were sitting at my kitchen table, waiting for Adrienne to come home from her first day at Brearley. Phoebe had a new set of romantic suspense posters (girls in off-the-shoulder peasant blouses hanging from cliffs, tied up in caves, disappearing down Alpine crevasses, getting swamped by tidal waves) and four different colors of AWR letterhead. Nick had the Personal Response Form for the Department of Social Services. I had given him a dollar and hired him as my lawyer.

"The key to it," I said, "was that she didn't know she'd sold the manuscript twice. She had it retyped and left the original on the receptionist's desk to be returned. But Jane Herman came along and thought she saw it in the In box, and had nothing to do for the weekend, and the next thing you know, Dana had sold it to Gallard Rowson as a Verna Train novel, and Jane had sold it to AST as a Sarah English novel. If Sarah hadn't come to New York, or hadn't had dinner with all of us, no one would have known until the books were published."

"Do you have any skin irregularities?" Nick asked.

"What?"

"Social services." He waved the forms in my face. "If you want to go through with this adoption, you've got to fill out two sets of forms. New York and Connecticut. Skin irregularities," he said again.

"No," I said. "She was completely out of control by the end, you know. Once the secret started getting out, it was *out*. She got Radd Stassen by doctoring his coffee when he came to tell her he'd found out about Max's ghosting, but she couldn't have stopped with him. She'd have had to waste half the business before she was safe. Maybe they will get her off on Extreme Emotional Disturbance. God only knows she had to be crazy to think she could pull it off."

"You have to be crazy to think you can pull this off," Nick said. "Listen to this. Religious involvement. What in the name of God do they want? Piety on a scale of one to ten? Contacts with Krishna groups? Membership in—"

"Protestant Episcopal," I said. "I think we're high church."

"You think?"

"I prefer high church," I said. "It's prettier."

"You're a Congregationalist," Phoebe said patiently. "It's your Aunt Eugenie who's Protestant Episcopal."

Nick glared at us.

Out in the hall, the apartment door opened and closed. The hall closet opened and closed. Adrienne appeared in the kitchen, prim and neat in Brearley's maroon and navy uniform. She put her books on the table and took a chair. We stared at her.

"Well," I said, "how was it?"

"I'll get you something to eat," Phoebe said. "I made cookies."

"Could I have some milk, please?" Adrienne said.

"Of course, milk," Phoebe said.

Adrienne turned to me. "You can wear any socks and shoes you want," she said. "Most of them have Adidases and funny knee socks. Courtney has reindeer knee socks."

"Who's Courtney?"

"Courtney Feinberg. She sits next to me."

"You like her?"

"A lot. She's very smart."

"Where does she get her knee socks?"

"Putumayo."

I winced. I couldn't tell Adrienne she couldn't go to Putumayo, since I go there myself. On the other hand, the prices . . .

Adrienne took three large cookies and bit one over her napkin. "Are we going to get married to Nick?" she said.

Nick looked at her, nodded, and stuck a thumb in the air. "You don't have to do that for free," he told her. "I'll pay you to talk her into it."

Adrienne ignored him. "If we're going to get married to Nick," she said, "we ought to do it right away. Before court." Court was what Adrienne called the adoption. She'd been all in favor of adoption since she'd found out she didn't have to change her name to do it. Staying Adrienne English was one of the things she was doing for her mother.

"I talked to Courtney, and she said with adoptions they like the adopting person to be married," she said. "So I think we should cover our—"

I gave her a look. She coughed. "You know what I mean," she said.

"That I do," I said.

"I think you're going to have to do this," Nick said gleefully. "I think she's going to back you into a corner."

"Nobody backs me into a corner," I said.

"Everybody backs you into corners," Nick said. "You spend your life getting backed into corners."

"Courtney says it's very important," Adrienne insisted.

"It would help," Nick pointed out.

"It would be good for you," Phoebe said.

"The next thing you're going to want is a move to the suburbs," I said.

Adrienne looked horrified. "Oh no," she said. "You never give up a good apartment in *Manhattan.*"

I was beginning to have second thoughts about Brearley. It was reputed to be the best girls' school in Manhattan, but I was beginning to think there was such a thing as being too bright. And too hip. If there was something like that, Adrienne was going to have it down in less than a week.

I grabbed a cookie and got out of my chair. Putumayo, for God's sake. Reindeer knee socks. Courtney Feinberg.

"Don't tell me," I said. "You want to be a flower girl."

"I'm too old to be a flower girl," Adrienne said. "But if that's what it takes to get you to do it, I'll do it."

Nick was grinning like a homicidal maniac. "Score," he said.

"Caterers," Phoebe said. "And not just the caterers. Invitations. I'll have to call Tiffany's. And the flowers, this time of year—"

After all that, buying a kid eighty-dollar sneakers actually seemed sane.